Won't Let You Down
The Cedarville Series #8
By
Bree Kraemer

Won't Let You Down

The Cedarville Series
Bree Kraemer
Published by Bree Kraemer, 2018.

Won't Let You Down

Also by Bree Kraemer
The Only Series
Only By His Touch
Only With Trust
If Only
Only You
Only For Love
Cedarville Novels
An Unexpected Home
Capturing Us
Choosing You
Better Together
A Chance Worth Taking
Forever Starts Here
After All These Years
Won't Let You Down
Say When
Something to Lose
Finally Home
Friends & Brothers
Sky High Love
Bridge To Love
When It's Love
Rockstar Romance
The Right Note
Pick Me
Christmas Novella
Light Me Up
DecorHATE for the Holidays
The Beckmeyer Family
Hooked
Sparked
Shocked
Kneaded
Valley Falls Strikers
Late Tackle
First Touch
Give & Go
Narrowing the Angle
He's a Keeper

Ground Rule
Walk Off
Sacrifice Bunt
Grand Slam (April 2023)

Chapter 1

Cramping hands. Sore back. And eyes that burned from the fumes of acetone.

As much as it all sucked, it also meant that it had been a good day.

At least in the life of a nail technician.

Joy stretched her neck as she walked to her car at the end of a long day. And it had been a long day. She'd started her day at nine and it was now twenty after eight. She'd had a one hour break around two, but other than that she'd worked straight through.

And now she was paying the price.

Long days were par for the course, especially in the summer, which was wedding season. Every bride, along with her bridesmaids, mother, mother-in-law, and the entire rest of her family, wanted her nails and toes gorgeous for the big day.

That's where Joy came in.

She was the best at what she did. Or so she'd been told hundreds of times over the last five years. And she liked it. Most days. She loved being a contractor and not an actual employee. If she was an employee, she'd have to see people she didn't want to see. Or walk-ins. But because she was a contractor, her clients came to her pretty much wherever she was. Sure, she took on new clients when they were referred by someone she trusted, or sometimes when the salon was packed and needed help. Those were usually the days she didn't love.

But, even on those days, she only hated her job like twenty percent of the time. That was pretty damn good in her book. She knew people who despised their jobs day in and day out yet still did them. That was no way to live.

It was a short drive to her apartment from the salon, even with her pit stop at the market to get some food. She hadn't had the chance to shop in over a week and she knew from breakfast that there was virtually no food in her kitchen.

A month ago it wouldn't have been a problem. Her roommate, Wes, had always kept the kitchen stocked and he'd even cooked. At least for the six weeks he'd lived there. But, now he was married to Julia and they were living with her mom while they decided what to do next. She was still shocked that he and Julia had gotten married so fast, but seeing how in love they were, it made complete sense. They were meant to be together and after so many years apart; she was happy they'd found their way back to love.

But damn, she missed his food. The man could cook, and what was worse, was that he enjoyed it. Sure, she could go to his restaurant, Dockside, if she really wanted his food, but she was saving all the money for the day that she could finally afford her own salon. And that meant no eating out, no shopping, no movies. Pretty much no social life.

Thankfully it was summer and she lived in a lake town where all her friends either had boats or access to them. Boats and swimming were virtually free entertainment making it easy on her pocketbook.

She shopped quickly, grabbing enough food to last for, hopefully, a few days. She didn't want to be doing this again tomorrow or the next day. Really, she didn't want to do it ever, but you know, that wasn't an option.

She was not what you'd call domestic. She hated things like cooking, organizing, cleaning and anything else that you'd expect women, especially mothers, to do. Not that she was a mother, but someday she'd like to be. Maybe. But her skills in homemaking were not going to win any awards.

She'd blame her mom, but she was done with that. She couldn't keep using her parents' deaths as excuses for everything that was bad in her life. She was a big girl – not in stature since she was barely five foot three – and needed to start owning up to her own mistakes.

Yes, her dad had died when she'd been young and left her mom with a huge debt. And yes, her mom had gotten cancer and died when she'd just gotten out of high school. For a while, she had used those events as reasons to not grow up, to throw caution to the wind and not think about the consequences of her actions. But no more.

When her sister, Avery had gotten hurt because of her, she'd vowed to change her ways. Even before Avery had been hurt, she'd been reflecting on her life, wondering if it was time to stop the sleeping around.

She wasn't proud of the fact that for years she'd go to bars to pick up guys. But, at the time, it had felt good to have someone want her. After a while, though, she'd started to feel more sad than happy. And eventually, she'd felt dirty. That's when she decided it was time to stop. And then Avery got attacked by a guy who thought she was Joy. He was angry that Joy had in one moment said yes, but in the next, changed her mind and said no.

She'd done that a lot those last few months. Leave the bar with a guy only to get to his place and back out. One day she had just woken up and decided that she couldn't sleep with all the guys anymore. That she wanted more. But she still felt lonely, so she continued to hit the bars and pick up guys. Only after dancing and making out, she couldn't go through with doing more. Then Avery got attacked, and that changed everything.

She had to stop.

Her actions had put the only person who loved her in danger, and that was unacceptable.

It was time to grow up and be an adult. And adults didn't sleep around with random guys every night. Or if they did, they didn't wake up feeling worse than they had.

It hadn't been as hard as she'd thought it was going to be. She'd moved to Cedarville and kept busy by taking a lot of jobs and spending her extra time with her sister. And in doing so, she made a lot of new friends in town. People she had come to like. Wes and Julia for example.

Grabbing the food she'd purchased at the market, she hurried inside before she broke an arm. She'd rather carry ten bags than make a second trip. Entering her apartment, which was on the first floor of a three-story, six-unit building, she was hit with a blast of hot, sticky air.

"What the fuck?" She dropped the bags on the counter and at once, checked the thermostat.

It was set to seventy but the temperature inside read eighty-four. She flipped it off and waited a few minutes before turning it back on. Nothing. She tried lowering the temperature. Nothing.

Groaning, she went back to the kitchen, found her phone and dialed the complex manager. Only it rang and rang and nobody answered. It did not allow her to leave a message.

After she put all her food away, she walked around the place and opened all the windows. Then she pulled out an old fan and positioned it at one end of the couch. After she made herself something to eat, she turned off all the lights since they caused too much heat, and sat down on the couch to eat while she watched TV.

She was sweating, but that was no surprise. It was mid-July in Ohio meaning the humidity was through the roof. Add to that, no air conditioning, and it was miserable. She tried the manager again. Still nothing.

His name was Carl, an older man maybe in his late sixties. When she'd moved in, he'd told her how he and his wife had purchased the building twenty years ago as an investment to help with their retirement. The place was nice and they'd kept up with updates and codes. That's why it was so weird to find the air not working.

If it wasn't so late, she would walk across the hall and ask her neighbor if hers was working. She couldn't remember her name and they'd met only once. So knocking on her door at nine o'clock at night was probably not a good idea.

She tried calling him again, and again it rang and rang. Giving up, she stripped off all her clothes and turned off the television. It was cooler out in the living room rather than in her bedroom, so she might as well sleep there. With any luck, maybe the air would kick on in the middle of the night.

But when she woke up in a pool of her own sweat, she knew that had been a pipe dream. Groaning, she grabbed her phone and once again tried Carl. Still nothing. This was seriously not right. She had the whole day off and now she wouldn't even be able to hang out at her own apartment.

Not that she was planning to stay there all day. She had plans to see Avery for at least a few hours, but now she'd have to find other things to do. No way was she staying in a hot apartment all day.

After a shower and a quick breakfast, she sent a text to Avery to see if she was awake. When she answered that she was, she grabbed her purse and keys and headed out the door. Surprisingly she ran into her neighbor in the hallway.

"Morning," Joy said.

"Hi." She always seemed so shy to Joy.

"Is your air conditioning working?"

"Yeah, it is."

"Then it must just be mine."

"You don't have air?" her neighbor said, her voice the loudest she'd ever heard it.

"No, and it really sucks." Joy bit her lip. "I'm really sorry but I forgot your name. I'm Joy." She extended her arm to shake her hand.

"Norah." She shook her hand. "I don't actually think I ever told you my name the last time we met."

"It doesn't matter. Now we know each other." She smiled and tried to put her at ease. She seemed so...nervous.

"Did you try calling the manager?"

"I did and his phone just keeps ringing and no voicemail picks up."

"Are you calling the new number?" Joy didn't remember getting a new number for Carl.

"When Carl sold the place he sent out info for the new owner."

"Carl sold the building?" She said it louder than she should have because Norah took a step back and her eyes went wide. "Sorry I didn't mean to yell, but I had no idea."

"Yeah, I think I got the letter a month or so ago."

That explained it. Wes probably got the info and hadn't told her. "Do you happen to have a new number?"

"Sure." Norah pulled out her phone and clicked through it. "Here it is. A Mr. Murray." She turned her phone towards Joy and Joy quickly typed the info into her own phone.

"Thank you. I appreciate it. I don't think I could sleep another night without air conditioning."

"I hope they fix it."

Joy waved and began walking away. "Have a good day."

In her car, with the air conditioning on high, she called the new number. It immediately went to voicemail with a generic voice telling her to leave a message. She left her name and number and what the problem was as nicely as possible. It wasn't unlike her to be blunt, and that was not the best way to sweeten up someone when you needed something fixed.

She threw her phone on the seat next to her and drove to Avery and Dax's house. They lived on the opposite side of town, back in a wooded area. Dax had built the house himself before he and Avery had ever met and it sat on a couple of acres of land. Avery had fallen in love with it almost as fast as she'd fallen in love with him. Joy had to admit though, it was a great house.

She was happy for her sister. Deliriously happy. But there was a part of her, a teeny tiny part that wished it was she who was happy and in love. A part that wished she had someone to lean on or a shoulder to cry on when things didn't go her way.

There was a bigger part of her though that wanted to make it on her own first before she fell in love. Even though she knew that falling in love was out of her hands. She was a huge believer in fate and soulmates. She knew without a doubt that there was one perfect person out there for her. And someday she would find him. Or maybe he would find her. Either way, she knew it would happen.

That was the only part of her that was optimistic. In the rest of her life she would categorize herself as a pessimist. Avery liked to say that wasn't true but Joy was a realist and knew herself well. If she didn't have expectations, she couldn't be let down.

Some might say that was a shitty way to live but it worked for her. Sometimes.

Then there were the times she secretly dreamed of things like her own salon. Or even her own house. A house she could raise a family in. Those were her secret optimistic thoughts that she never told anyone about.

Well, except for the salon. She'd spilled the beans on that to her sister one night while they were drinking and now everyone seemed to know about it. But she was okay with that because it made things easier when she said she couldn't do something because she was saving money.

Pulling into Avery's driveway, she didn't see Dax's work truck, so she assumed he was gone for the day. When she got to the door, Avery opened it before she could even knock and their brand new puppy, Thunder, came barrelling out.

She couldn't stop herself from bending down to pet and snuggle with the adorable puppy. "Hey boy," she ruffled his baby-soft fur, "who's the cutest puppy ever?"

"Cute is his only redeeming quality." Avery had her hands on her hips, an angry frown on her face. "He keeps eating everything he can find."

"That's not your fault, buddy." She let him lick her face. "Mommy and Daddy shouldn't leave their things out where you can reach them, should they?"

"Sure, take his side."

Joy stood, bringing Thunder with her under her arm. "He's just a baby and he's still learning." Carrying Thunder she walked into the house. Avery followed them and once the door was shut, Joy set Thunder back on the floor. "Go play, but be good." He bounced off, practically tripping over his own feet. "You know he's going to be giant right?"

"Yeah but that's what we wanted. Although sometimes I think we might have bitten off more than we can chew."

"You'll get the hang of it."

"It'll be easier once we get the fence up, which will hopefully be tonight."

"You guys are putting in a fence today?"

"Well, Dax and Flynn are putting in a fence. I will be helping with whatever I can."

Hearing Flynn's name had her whole body on alert. It was frustrating and she hated it. She did not like that damn man.

Or so she told herself every time she saw him.

"Do you guys need some help? I can't go home so I might as well stay here."

"Why can't you go home?" Avery walked to the couch and sat down.

"My air conditioning isn't working. It's like a hundred degrees in there."

"Did you call someone?"

"Yeah but last night I had the old number and didn't find out until this morning that there was a new owner with a new number."

"You slept there last night with no air conditioning?" Avery's voice was incredulous.

"It was fine, Avery. A little heat never killed anyone."

"Wrong. It absolutely can kill you. It was over ninety degrees out yesterday. Temps that high can cause breathing problems."

"In old people or kids. Of which I am neither." She rolled her eyes at her sister.

"You are staying here tonight and until it is fixed. And don't even think of arguing."

"I'm a big girl and I can take care of myself. I don't need my sister always bailing me out." It had been that way forever and she didn't want to be a burden any longer.

"I'm not bailing you out. The air conditioning in your apartment isn't working, which isn't your fault. I am offering you a place to stay until the owner can get it fixed. That's the human thing to do."

Joy pursed her lips, understanding what her sister was saying. "All right, but know I am doing this under protest."

"I know how hard you are working to make it on your own and not rely on other people, but Joy, this is just common sense."

She hung her head. She knew Avery only wanted to help her and now she felt bad for sounding like an ingrate. "You're the best sister ever, Ave's, don't think I don't know that."

"Only second best to you." Her smile was so genuine and so happy. "Now come out back and I'll show you what else we are thinking of doing aside from just the fence."

Joy followed her sister through the house and out onto the deck with Thunder on their heels. As soon as she looked outside, her thoughts drifted to Flynn. There was something about the man that she couldn't put her finger on. He rarely spoke to her, but if they were in the same room, the looks he gave her were long and intense. And each time she saw him, she would have visions of things that didn't make any sense. Like a song would pop into her head or a scene from a movie.

She had no idea why nor did she know why she had such a strong sexual reaction to him. Was he gorgeous? Uh yeah, that was a no brainer. He was tall, broad-shouldered, and built like a linebacker. His unkempt hair was longer around his ears, but the pièce de résistance was his beard.

Oh God, his beard.

She had never been someone who loved facial hair. It was the opposite. It usually grossed her out thinking about all the germs in there. But on Flynn, holy shit, her fingers itched to run through it and that was just the clean version of what she wanted to do. Images of his head between her legs was the dirty version, and man, did she long for the dirty version.

That might have more to do with her lack of sex and less to do with him.

But, probably not.

Why did she tell her sister she would stay and help? Now she would have to see him all day and work next to him.

Oh yeah, that's exactly why she'd volunteered to help.

She was no dummy.

Chapter 2

"Why did I offer to help you again?" Flynn was loading lumber into Dax's truck so he could help him build a fence at his house.

"Because you are a damn good friend." He hefted more boards up and onto the truck. "And, because you know I'll have beer and food waiting for you."

He couldn't deny either of those things, not to mention spending a Saturday working with his best friend was better than sitting at home alone.

Not that he minded being alone. He'd gotten used to it over the years. Work was his life and that was fine by him. He went out enough to have a social life, and occasionally he even met a nice woman. And sure, it had been more months than he could count since he'd actually done either of those things, but who cared. It wasn't like he was a hermit who never saw people like Dax had been only months ago.

Dax had been a professional workaholic before he'd met Avery. The man had worked twelve-hour days at a minimum and never went out. Ever. No joke. Then one day he walked onto a job and saw her, and that was it for him.

Flynn was envious. He'd been open his whole life to falling in love, and yet, it never came.

Maybe there was something wrong with him.

He rubbed his beard, shaking his head.

This damn beard. The one he'd grown back out again after months without it. The one he'd sworn he'd never have again.

The one he only had because of a crazy woman who once told him she liked it, before leaving and then, seemingly, forgetting all about him.

"Are you gonna daydream all day or are you gonna help me load this truck?"

Shaking off images of a blonde beauty who infuriated him beyond belief, he once again began loading the truck.

"Any clue on when you and Avery are going to get married?" They'd gotten engaged over a month ago and he'd yet to hear his friend say anything about the wedding.

"Funny thing about that." He stopped loading, putting his hands on his hips. "We had said we were going to go away for a weekend and just elope, but after Wes and Julia got married with only a few days' notice, Avery decided that's what she wanted. And I agree."

"What does that mean?"

"It means that next weekend, in our backyard, we are getting married."

"Seriously?" Flynn wasn't so much shocked as happy. Dax and Avery were perfect for each other.

"Yup. Mark your calendar for next Saturday at four."

"I'll be there. I'm so happy for you, man." Dax had hired him with no experience when he was just a twenty-year-old kid and from there they had become friends. Best friends. And now his best friend was getting married. There was no way he was missing that. "If you need any help, I'm your man."

"This fence and the gazebo we are building are all I need."

"Gazebo? I thought we were just doing a fence?"

"Uh yeah, the gazebo was a last-minute addition. I've always wanted one, and with the wedding, this seems like the perfect time."

"So the two of us are going to put up a fence and build a gazebo? In just two days?"

"Avery will be there to help, and she just texted and said that Joy is there too. It won't just be us."

Joy.

The beard loving, blonde beauty who drove him insane.

Just what he needed.

Not that he minded seeing her. On the contrary. He always seemed to want to see her. But, her lack of interest in him was really starting to grate. It's like she had no memory of him. Some days he wondered if he'd dreamed the whole thing up.

It was over six months ago, right after Christmas, at a bar in Woodridge. He was eating alone at a table in the back. The place wasn't busy, in fact, when he'd walked in, he was one of only five or six people there. He was halfway through his meal when he looked up and saw her walk in. Gorgeous, even if she was a little underdressed for December. Her blonde hair was down and around her face, and her eyes were bright blue and shining.

He couldn't take his eyes off her. And then she spotted him, and her smile lit up the whole room, even as she stalked toward him. He knew she was on the prowl, looking to pick up a guy. But that didn't seem to matter. He was drawn to her in a way that he'd never been with another woman.

As she approached him, he worked hard to control his erratic heartbeat. He didn't want to come off as too eager.

They exchanged pleasantries, but soon, she began coming on to him. He couldn't stop himself from calling a halt. He said something to the effect of, drop the act and let's just have a good time talking. Her face fell, but only for a second, before she sat down and sighed. She apologized for coming on so strong, saying that meeting new people was so hard.

For almost two hours they talked about everything. She was direct and didn't really hold anything back. They talked about their jobs and their favorite things.

He knew her favorite song, Come Over by Kenny Chesney, and her favorite movie, Mean Girls. He knew she never drank coffee, instead opting for a soda, if she needed a morning pick me up. She hated working out but did yoga several times a week because she enjoyed how it relaxed her. She didn't cook or clean, even though she someday wanted kids and had no idea how she'd make it as a mom without those things.

The comment that affected him the most though, was when she'd told him that normally she hated beards, but on him, it worked. And then she ran her fingers through it. He'd stilled as her small hand caressed the hair on his chin, her fingers lightly grazing his skin underneath. When she realized what she was doing, she pulled her hand away at the speed of light and excused herself to go to the bathroom.

And then she never came back.

He'd waited for twenty minutes, like an idiot, before finally getting up and leaving. He'd been so deflated after that. He'd thought they had a real connection and had planned to get her number and ask her out.

He'd gone back to that same bar a dozen more times in search of her, but she never showed up. He felt like such a fool. He'd even asked the bartender, who had told him that she normally came in several times a week. But, after their night together, he'd never seen her again.

Until the night he went out with Dax and Dan in March. She'd walked right up to the three of them and hit on them. All of them. Not caring which one she ended up with. Not only that, but she didn't seem to recognize him.

Sure she'd been drunk, or close to it, and he'd no longer had his beard, but he didn't think either of those things made him unforgettable. After that—and once he found out that Joy was Avery's sister—he grew the beard back. He wanted her to remember him on her own.

He hadn't seen her that often since that night, maybe a half dozen times, but each time, he wasn't able to look away. He was mesmerized by her even after she'd walked out on him.

And now he was going to get to spend the whole day working side-by-side with her.

Maybe his luck was changing.

Once the trucks were loaded, they each drove to Dax's house and immediately began unloading the materials. On his second trip back to the truck, he found Joy and Avery pulling wood from the truck.

"Hey, Flynn," Avery greeted him. "Thanks for helping out."

He tore his eyes from Joy to look at her. "No problem. Dax told me the good news."

She lit up like a firework. "I hope you can make it. It's really just our friends and family. Very similar to Wes and Julia's."

He'd gone to Wes and Julia's wedding, and it had been casual and fun. He had no doubt that Dax and Avery's would be the same. Avery took off with her arms loaded, leaving him alone with Joy.

"Do you need some help?" Those might have been the first words he'd said to her in months.

She shook her head and turned away from him. Boards in hand, she walked away.

Fuck.

Could that have been more awkward?

He began gathering more wood in his arms trying to figure out a way to have an actual conversation with Joy. But, how could he do that when she wouldn't even talk to him?

Although she did stare at him. A lot.

He'd caught her on several occasions, but when she found him looking toward her, she would quickly turn her head.

Did that mean something?

Maybe he should try a different tactic. She was known for her brash attitude so, maybe instead of being nice, he should give her some of her own medicine.

Carrying his boards around to the back, he dropped them in the pile with the others. Dax had already cut all the boards to size at the shop and had also dug all the holes and set the posts. Today was all about the boards and wire.

Oh, and the gazebo.

Dax came to stand next to him. "I've got the gazebo plans in the garage. I thought we could get Avery and Joy started on the fence and you and I can go start that."

"Sounds good." Just then, Thunder, their brand new puppy came barreling toward them. Dax bent down to pet him and then looked up at Flynn.

"Do you mind getting them started? I'm going to feed this guy and take him on a quick walk, hopefully, it will tire him out."

"You got it." Both Avery and Joy came up behind them.

"We're ready to work," Avery said. While she looked happy about it, Joy did not. She even looked a little annoyed.

Dax walked away, and he started to show them how they would screw the boards into the posts. They both caught on quickly, and while he wanted to be more blunt or pushy with Joy, he just couldn't. At least not with Avery right there.

After they'd each done two boards on their own, Flynn felt confident that they were good to go on by themselves. He went ahead of them and measured out the spacing so they could just screw the boards in without having to stop. After several boards, Dax poked his head out the door and yelled to Avery that he needed help with something.

That left him alone with Joy.

He wasn't sure whether to be happy or scared.

Moving over so he could help her, he stayed silent as he held the board so she could screw it in.

After finishing one whole board, they both squatted down to do the middle one. Not able to work in silence he said, "It's nice of you to help out." He looked over to where she was screwing in the board.

"It's better than being at my hot apartment."

"What's that now?" He stood as she finished screwing it in.

"The air is out in my apartment, so it's super hot in there."

"Did you call your landlord?"

She gave him a *do I look stupid* look. "Yes I did."

"I was just asking. No need to get testy."

She sighed, just like she had done the night she sat down with him at the bar. God it was sexy and went right to his groin. "I don't mean to be an ass, it was just a bad night."

"You don't have to apologize to me. I'm sorry if I came off as thinking you weren't smart enough to call your landlord."

They both moved over to start the next row of boards.

"I could come look at it for you if you want. Electrical is my specialty."

She looked up at him and gave him a half-smile. "Why would you do that?"

"Friends help each other out."

"But we aren't really friends."

Well hell, that stung. "All right, acquaintances then. Either way, people around here help each other."

"I'm not super big on accepting help. Anyway, the building manager will take care of it."

Okay. There went trying to be nice. Thank God Dax and Avery chose that moment to come back outside. He let Avery take over for him and he went with Dax into the garage.

"What did you say to Joy to give her that scowl?" Dax asked.

"Apparently offering to look at her broken air conditioning was a no-no."

"Ah, Avery told me about that. I can't believe she slept there last night with it being that hot in there. She must have been miserable."

"She slept there?" He stopped walking. That was insane. It had been over ninety degrees yesterday and inside an apartment it would have been even hotter.

Dax stopped and turned to look at him. "That's what Avery said. She's staying here tonight though, so at least there's that."

Flynn had to get it together. She wasn't his to worry about. "That's good." He began walking again.

Together they poured over the designs for the gazebo making sure it would stand not only for the wedding but also for years to come. They built the frame right in the garage, so they could easily cut pieces to the correct sizes. When it was ready, they carried it out back to where it would stand.

"Oh my God," Avery screamed. "Look at how big it's going to be." She came running over to where they'd set it down. "You said it was going to be small."

"I lied." Dax grabbed her around the waist and gave her a quick kiss. "My girl gets only the best."

"You're the best." This time she kissed him.

Flynn looked away as they embraced, and when he did, he caught sight of Joy. She was standing several feet away with her arms crossed and a smile on her face.

She looked happy.

And that was rare.

She'd looked that way the night they'd sat at a table in the back of the bar talking. And ever since, he couldn't get her out of his mind.

Her head turned, her eyes connecting with his. Instead of turning away like she usually did, she held his gaze. Several emotions washed over his body, but the dominant one was want.

He wanted her.

Fiercely.

Unfortunately, he couldn't decipher the expression on her face, but he had to assume by her steady gaze, that she didn't despise him as much as she liked to pretend she did.

Or, maybe he was just delusional.

"Let's get going," Dax said as he walked over to him. "The sooner we finish this the sooner you can go home."

Suddenly going home was the last thing he wanted to do.

They worked hard until lunch where they ate sandwiches outside while Thunder ran around trying to steal their food. Avery and Joy were inside most of the time, Dax saying they were working on wedding stuff. After they ate, he and Dax finished the fence since that was needed the most so that Thunder could run around without running away. It was after three when they finished that and started back on the gazebo. They hadn't seen Avery or Joy, but when he went in to use the bathroom, he passed them both in the kitchen.

"How's it going?" Avery asked.

"Pretty good. We are working on the roof of the gazebo now." They had moved fast, but that was always the way with them. They worked well together and always had.

"You're the best, Flynn. Thanks for helping."

He nodded and flicked his eyes to Joy. She wasn't looking at him, instead, her head was down as she flipped through a magazine. As he walked to the hallway, he wondered again how she couldn't remember him. The beard he had grown back after the night she tried to pick him – and his two friends – up at a bar, should make him more recognizable as the guy she'd had a two-hour conversation with.

He didn't know much about her but that was his own fault. He'd never asked Dax, because he didn't want his best friend of ten years to have any suspicion that he had a thing for his, soon to be, sister-in-law.

He wasn't sure why that was though. Dax wouldn't care. Probably.

But if he did, Flynn would have no choice but to choose his friend over a woman.

Even Joy. A woman he thought about more than he'd ever thought of any other.

Back outside, they worked for another two hours before calling it quits. There were just a few small things left to do on the gazebo, but Dax was going to do them himself the next day. As they walked up to the deck, Avery was standing there, offering them each a beer.

"Pizza will be here soon." She sat down at the table where Joy was already sitting, sipping her own beer.

"I think we did well for one day of work." Dax spread his legs out in front of him and took a sip of his beer.

"It really is a work of art. Great job on the design."

"I've been working on it for weeks. Avery kept saying she didn't care about the size, but with our large yard, I wanted something we could use for parties or kids, or really, whatever."

Kids. Wow. He knew his friend was planning for the future, but hearing him talk about kids was weird. It wasn't that long ago that he'd buried himself in work and had no social life. Then, as if with the flip of a switch, he was in a relationship, getting married and talking about starting a family.

Life really was crazy.

He tilted his head and out of the corner of his eye he could see Joy. She had her feet propped up on the table and she was leaning back laughing at something Avery said. Her hair was now down and flowing freely in the summer breeze around her face.

The way she made him feel, the way he felt about her, he couldn't help but to wonder if she was his switch.

Was she the one who was supposed to be his? Was she his forever?

And if she was, how in the hell did he go about finding out when she barely spoke to him?

Chapter 3

There was still no word from the new apartment manager and Joy was starting to get pissed. While she didn't mind spending time with her sister, she hated being a burden.

They'd had dinner, Flynn had left—thank God—and she was now snuggled comfortably in the guest room, nice and cool in the air conditioning.

Before she'd laid down, she'd left another message about her broken unit. It was getting kind of ridiculous that the new manager hadn't gotten back to her and she planned to have a few words with him, if and when he ever contacted her.

She'd like to blame him for her strange awkwardness with Flynn, but that was all on her. Or maybe, it was his fault for always staring at her.

Why did he always stare at her?

And why, for fuck's sake, did she feel like she knew him?

Each and every time she'd looked at him that day, the feeling had gotten stronger. So strong, that at one point, she had a visual memory of touching the skin on his face.

But that was impossible.

Wasn't it?

She had no memory of ever coming into physical contact with him. Unless...

No she couldn't have. Could she?

Sitting up, she threw the covers off her body and swung her legs over the edge of the bed.

Had he been someone she'd picked up in a bar and taken home? Oh God, had she slept with him?

Dropping her head to her hands, she racked her brain hard for any memory she could dig up. She knew she'd hit on him the same night she hit on Dax, before he and Avery had gotten together. But, she only knew that because Dax had mentioned he was with him that night. That was one of her last nights of bar hopping, and even before that, she'd stopped sleeping with guys she picked up.

Sure, she'd made out with a few here and there and let them buy her drinks, but somewhere in the last year, sleeping with strangers had gotten old.

But what if before that, Flynn had been one of the guys? That would explain the looks, and him wanting to come by to check out her air conditioning.

He wanted a repeat performance.

Holy fuck.

Standing, she walked to the window to look out. The moon was full in the sky, lighting up the whole front of the house where her window faced. She stayed there, trying once again to place Flynn.

Only there was nothing.

She must have slept with him, only she had a hard time imagining that he was that forgettable. Flynn didn't strike her as the kind of wham bam thank you kind of guys she had been with. When she thought of him, she thought of slow, careful, seduction that took all night and left her boneless.

Not that she ever thought of him.

Nope. Never.

Sighing, because her head hurt from thinking about the possibility that she'd already ruined something good during a past that she was trying to forget, she sat back down on the bed.

What was it about Flynn that had her all up in her own head? He was hot, yes. Julia likened him to a lumberjack once, and she wasn't far off. She'd seen him in flannel more than once, and man, could the guy wear flannel.

But it was more than his looks. There was something else, something she couldn't put her finger on.

Fingers. Beard. Touching his beard with her fingers.

There it was again, a flash of what felt like a real memory. A fucking hot memory. A memory she wished was real, and that if it was real, that she could remember the whole thing.

Groaning, she rolled over and pulled the covers tighter around her. Being a fuck up was what she was known for, and it looked like nothing had changed.

She woke to her phone ringing and sleepily reached for it. It was the same number she'd called several times the day before for her building manager.

"Hello," she said, as awake as she could.

"Ms. Davies, this is Wyatt Murray, the new manager of the building you live in."

"Nice to finally hear from you, Mr. Murray."

"I'm sorry about that. I was out of touch all day yesterday and well, I have no excuse. I am sorry. But if it's okay, I'd like to come by now and check on the air conditioning?"

Hmm, a man who didn't offer excuses. That was new. "Sure. I'm not there though."

"No problem, I have the master if you are okay with me going in?"

"Please do."

"I will get back to you and let you know what is wrong and when it will be fixed."

"Thank you."

She hung up wondering if she was in an alternate universe. The guy had been so nice and apologetic. From what she knew of men, that wasn't normal. And sure, he'd been in the wrong, going a whole day and not answering her calls, but still.

After getting up and having breakfast with Avery and Dax, she headed back to her apartment. When she walked inside the first-floor lobby, she found her door cracked and light humming coming from inside. Pushing the door open, she announced herself.

"Hello."

From a crouched position in the hallway, inside the closet that housed her air, a man stood. "Oh hi, you must be Miss Davies. I'm Wyatt Murray."

"Sorry to just barge in, but I needed some things and I thought I'd see how it was going." The man was good looking even though he looked like he was barely out of high school. A cute little smile tipped the corner of his mouth and his dark hair was cropped so short it almost didn't look like he had hair.

"No problem. It's your place after all."

She walked in closer. He wasn't as tall as she had assumed from her doorway. Up close he was barely six feet. But it was six feet of hotness. Muscles flexed under his t-shirt, and his legs and ass filled out his jeans nicely. And he didn't look as young once she saw him face-to-face. "What's the verdict?"

"Looks like you will need a whole new unit. This one is shot."

"How long will that take?" She did not want to have to bother Avery by staying at her house any longer than necessary. Especially with her wedding only a week away.

"Not totally sure. I need to check with my brother and see when he can get here."

"Your brother?"

"Yeah, he and I run this place together."

She sighed. She did not need to know this guy's—hot or not—life history. What she wanted was to have her apartment back. Thankfully, the temperature had cooled a little and it was only going to be in the low to mid-eighties for the next few days. She'd be able to handle that, she hoped.

"Okay, just let me know when you find out."

He gathered up his tools and then started walking to the door. "Sorry again for the delay. Once this is all set, we can talk about a rent discount for your inconvenience."

She was stunned at his offer. She'd never had a landlord who was so accommodating. "I'd appreciate it."

After she closed the door behind him, she went and opened all the windows. She'd closed them when she'd left the day before because she lived on the first floor and didn't want anyone to break in. The fan she owned was still on, and she plugged in the one she was borrowing from Avery, in her bedroom. Once the air was circulating in her place, she started on some laundry. She had promised Julia that she would meet her for lunch at Dockside around noon. Dockside was the restaurant that Julia's husband, still crazy to say, and her friend, Wes, owned.

Because her own nails were horrible from the manual labor the day before, she gave herself a manicure, then said, what the fuck, and did her toes too. After they were dry, she cleaned up, changed clothes, and then transferred her clothes she'd washed to the dryer. She hated to use it, because it would heat the place up, but she had no choice. Because she only planned to be gone for a bit, she left her windows open when she left, even though it was against her better judgment.

Months ago, when she'd lived with Avery, they'd been robbed and virtually everything that they'd owned had been stolen. Not that they'd had much in the way of nice items, but it still stung to lose all her things. Now she was more careful, and always made sure the doors and windows were locked when she was out.

The drive to Dockside was quick, it was only a few streets over, and she found Julia sitting at the bar.

"Hey," she said, as she saddled up next to her and pulled out an empty stool.

"Oh good, you can be the deciding vote. Tell Sabrina she has to go out with the hot guy who asked her out." Sabrina was the bartender at Dockside. She was young, brash, and knew her shit.

Joy liked her.

"Hello," Sabrina said, "since when does my vote count less in decisions in my life?"

Julia waved her off. "You don't know what's good for you and need an outside point of view."

"Can I ask to be left out of this?" Joy made a face letting them both know she did not want to be involved.

"No you can't." Julia turned toward her. "We all need a push every now and again to get out of our funks. If Leah and Avery hadn't pushed me, I would have never gone out on a date with a guy who brought me here. And then I would have never reconnected with Wes. That date, as awful as it was, is what got me to this happy place."

"It's hard to argue with that logic," Joy said to Sabrina. "Tell me about the guy?"

"There's nothing to tell. He came in here Friday night. After several hours of him hanging at the bar, eating and drinking, he asked me out. I told him definitively that I don't date my customers."

"Is he cute?"

"Very."

"Nice?" She liked as much info as possible when helping out a friend.

"Yeah, sure. He was nice. We chatted as much as we could and from what I could tell he isn't an ax murderer."

"But you still don't want to date him?"

Sabrina sighed and dropped her elbows to the counter. "I just...I'm not a fan of dating someone I meet while I'm working."

"You've been burned," Julia guessed.

"More than once and honestly, it's just not worth it to try again."

Joy understood. "Then I think you should stick to your rule. Plus, when the right one comes, whether he's a customer or not, you'll know."

Sabrina laughed. "Any idea on when that might be? Maybe a time frame or year?"

"If I knew that, do you think I'd be single?" She rolled her eyes.

"It'll happen for both of you," Julia said. "I know it will."

Joy looked over to Sabrina. "She's so damn optimistic isn't she?"

"It used to be annoying," Sabrina said, "but now I think it's starting to rub off."

Before they could keep talking, a group of people took seats at the bar and Sabrina headed off to wait on them.

Julia turned to look at her. "I received my wedding invitation yesterday." Julia's eyes were bright, a smile so big that Joy thought her face might break. "Did Wes and I start a new tradition?"

"Looks like."

"I couldn't be happier for those two. And I'm glad, that even though it's an impromptu ceremony, that they are doing something. It never felt right to me that they were just going to elope."

"Avery said almost the same thing. She decided that even if everyone couldn't make it, at least a good portion of their friends and family would be there. You should see the gazebo that Dax built her. It's straight out of a movie."

"I can't wait to see it. Wes really wanted to help but, as you can see, this place doesn't allow for much free time." The place was busy. When she'd come in, only the bar had been dead, but both the inside tables and outside were full. Now the bar was the same way.

"He had help. I was there and so was Flynn." She said it as casually as possible hoping that Julia wouldn't think anything of it.

She was wrong.

"Flynn, as in the Flynn you want to do?"

"Keep your voice down," she shushed her. "And I do not want to do him."

She pursed her lips, a smile showing from underneath. "Lie to me all you want, but you can't lie to yourself."

She'd been doing just that for months and it was working out just fine for her. "I'm not lying. Totally. He just irritates me."

"You know it's a thin line between love and hate right?"

"I don't hate him. I just…" she looked around and lowered her voice. "Every time he is near I have what I can only describe as memories of him."

"Sexual memories?"

"No, that's the weird thing. I thought maybe I had slept with him and just didn't remember, but the only one I have of touching him, is running my fingers through his beard and my fingertips grazing his chin. The rest are things like movies or songs. Even some that seem like childhood memories."

"Have you guys ever talked about those things?"

"No, I've said a dozen words to him in total until yesterday. At least I think." The whole thing made her head hurt.

"Hmm." She tapped her fingers on the bar. "I'm wondering if you have some kind of repression going on."

"So I what, I slept with him, and then because it was so bad, I pushed it down deep to try to forget about it?"

"First, I didn't say you slept with him. Maybe you just talked to him. And second, what if it was so good and that's why you repressed it? People don't just try to ignore the bad things in their lives. They also do the same for good things."

She bit her lip. Could that have been it? Was sex with Flynn so amazing that she'd wanted to forget it? If you went by looks alone, Flynn was definitely good at sex. But, was she so fucked up that she would forget it?

"Again, I really don't think you had sex with him."

"So how do I find out?"

"Well, you could start by asking him?"

"Nope," she said immediately, "that's out."

Julia laughed. "Then the second option would be to work through it and find out why you are having these memories. I'd be glad to help you."

"Is that against protocol or anything? You helping a friend?"

"Nah. We wouldn't do it at the office and I wouldn't prescribe you any drugs. Just some general talking and stuff."

Could she talk to her friend about her past and all the crappy stuff she'd done?

Julia must have sensed her hesitation. "Or, if you want, I can talk to a colleague and see if they can talk to you. I don't want you to be uncomfortable."

"I'm not uncomfortable. What we talk about, is that just between you and me?"

"Yes, just because we won't be in my office and you won't be paying me doesn't mean you don't have doctor-patient privilege." She put her hand over Joy's. "You can tell me anything and I will never tell anyone."

She let out a breath, one she felt like she'd been holding onto forever. It wasn't just her Flynn memories she needed to work through. She'd been holding onto a lot over the course of her life, and maybe it was finally time to let it all go.

Sabrina stepped back in front of them, sliding two drinks across the bar. "You guys ordering food?"

"Mac and cheese and fries please," Joy said.

"I'll just have a grilled chicken salad. And can you tell Wes to add some extra chicken please?"

"You got it."

"You said you talked to Flynn yesterday. What did you talk about?"

"Is this my first session, Doc?" She knew she sounded snotty but sometimes she just couldn't help herself.

"No this is just your friend wondering what you and a hot guy talked about."

Joy laughed, feeling good. "He offered to fix my air conditioning when he found out it was broken."

"Your air conditioning isn't working? Since when?"

"Since Friday night. Or, probably Friday during the day sometime."

"Tell me you didn't stay there?"

"You know, just because you're older than me doesn't mean you're my mom."

"Call me your mom again and I will punch you."

They both laughed and again it felt good. "I stayed there Friday but spent all day yesterday with Avery and then stayed at her place."

"What about tonight?"

"It's a lot cooler and now I have a couple of fans. I'll be fine."

"You do know you can stay with us if you need to. We have plenty of room and my mom would probably love to fuss over you."

Humbled by the generosity of her friend, she looked down at the bar. "Thank you, and while I appreciate it, I think I am good. At least if it gets up and running in the next few days."

They talked until their food came and then after eating, decided to shop for new outfits for Avery's wedding. This was one thing she didn't mind spending money on.

Avery had asked her to be her maid of honor and Joy wanted to look good standing beside her sister. Not bride good, but good enough so that a certain rugged lumberjack might not be able to take his eyes off her.

She really did have issues.

Chapter 4

Flynn was two beers into his Sunday afternoon of relaxation when his phone rang. He didn't want to answer. Had no desire to talk to anyone, but when he flipped his phone over and saw his brother's face, he reluctantly answered.

"This better be good." He loved his brother, really he did. But today he wasn't in the mood to talk to him.

They weren't biological brothers since they'd both been adopted. But, they were as close as any biological brothers he'd ever seen. He'd been three when he was adopted and then five years later, his adopted parents brought Wyatt home. He'd been four and scared shitless. At least that's how Flynn remembered it.

He wouldn't talk to anyone, well, except for him. Somehow, he attached himself to Flynn and for weeks, he wouldn't eat or sleep unless Flynn was next to him. So began their lifelong friendship.

Flynn loved him and had always protected him, not that he needed it. He'd been a kid that everyone seemed to like. Flynn swore it was his eyes. They were friendly and made him likable. Plus, he had Hollywood good looks. Strong jaw, good cheekbones and a nose that somehow even though it was crooked made him look distinguished.

"Any chance you can be available to put in a new AC unit in the next day or so."

This made Flynn sit up. "What are you talking about?"

"One of the apartments in the building needs a new one."

Six months ago, they'd gone in together to purchase an apartment building. Wyatt contributed seventy percent. He only put in thirty with the understanding that he'd do any and all the maintenance work that would be needed.

Wyatt wasn't handy. At all. But, he had money from his few years as a stockbroker and playing the market. He was pretty much a math genius and had a way with numbers. After several years in New York, he'd come to Ohio saying that he no longer wanted to be a suit. So, Flynn had gone in on the investment with him, hoping to help his brother out.

And now an AC unit was out at the same time the woman he couldn't stop thinking about was without hers.

This could not be a coincidence.

"What's the name of the renter?"

"Why does that matter?"

"Wyatt, just tell me the name?"

"Joy Davies."

Holy shit. It was Joy.

"Why the hell didn't you call me first thing? You can't have people with no AC in this heat."

"Whoa, man, I didn't find out until this morning. What's this woman to you, anyway?"

"What do you mean you didn't find out until this morning? Her air was out on Friday night."

"I don't know but the first time she called me was yesterday around nine in the morning. I didn't get the messages until this morning. I," he paused, "I turned my phone off, like I sometimes do, and I just forgot to turn it back on."

Wyatt was notorious for turning his phone off and blocking out the world, but when they'd gone into this venture together, he'd promised he would always keep it on.

"Wyatt, you have to keep your phone on when you have tenants in a building who are relying on you."

"Stop with the lecture okay. I already feel bad enough about it. Are you ever going to tell me how you know her?"

"She's Avery's twin sister."

"Avery, as in Dax's girlfriend?"

"Yeah. Actually, as of next Saturday she'll be Dax's wife."

"Okay, this is a lot of info. Dax is getting married and you have a thing for his soon to be wife's twin sister?"

"I don't have a thing for her." His voice was more defensive than he wanted.

"She's hot by the way. I thought about hitting on her myself when I was there, except I promised myself I wouldn't date any tenants."

He wanted to punch his brother for even looking at Joy and that thought, that one little thought, said a lot about how he felt about her.

But, he couldn't deal with that right this second. First, he had to get her air conditioning working. "Send me the unit size and info. I will order one immediately."

"I'll do it right now. If you could let me know when it's ready and when you can put it in, I promised I'd give her a heads up."

"I'll do it. You stay away from her."

Wyatt laughed. "It's like that, is it?"

Flynn practically growled, "Send me her info," and hung up. Seconds later, his phone dinged with the info he needed on the unit and her number. He pushed Wyatt's words from his mind and called up his best supplier for AC units. He had a buddy who worked there and, hopefully, with any luck, he could get one in a day.

After a little haggling, his friend agreed to a good price and said he had a unit in stock. Flynn figured he could grab it first thing in the morning and, maybe by the end of the day Tuesday, he'd have it all finished. Dax would gladly give him the time if need be, but the more he thought about it the more he hated Joy going any longer than needed without air.

Shaking his head because he was a damn fool, he changed into work clothes before driving to the shop to get a work truck and tools. He'd texted Dax to make sure it was okay, leaving out that it was Joy's apartment he'd be working on.

After getting the truck, he ran by and picked up the AC unit. Wyatt was meeting him at Joy's, passing off the key so he'd be able to enter and exit. He still hadn't contacted Joy to tell her he was the one who would be fixing her air. Honestly, he was kinda just hoping she'd be there when he showed up so he didn't have to make an awkward phone call.

Only, he wasn't that lucky. Wyatt was already there, but Joy was nowhere to be found.

"You really want to start this now? It's already after three."

"Yeah well, if I can get a decent amount finished tonight then I will only miss one day of work." That was half true. It was more that he didn't want Joy to wait. And also that he wanted to see her.

He always wanted to see her.

"Suit yourself."

"Can you do me a favor, text Joy and let her know someone is here working. Only," he stopped what he was doing and looked at his brother, "don't tell her it's me."

"That depends, are you going to tell me what's up with you and her?"

"Not today I'm not. Give me some time to see if it turns into something." God, he hoped it turned into something.

Wyatt lifted an eyebrow in understanding. "I'll call her now. And Flynn, if she isn't into you, she's an idiot. You are the best person I know."

Flynn softened. "Back at ya."

He began to unload his truck of the tools he'd need and as he brought them inside, he took in her living space. It was small and cluttered with clothes, magazines and books. There were a few dishes in the sink, but otherwise, the place was clean. He was no neat freak himself, so he wasn't one to talk about how other people lived.

"It's done," Wyatt said, as he walked back into Joy's apartment. "I told her someone would be here tonight and again most of the day tomorrow. She said that's fine and that she would be home in a couple of hours."

He nodded. "Thanks. Now help me carry the unit in here." He'd need it outside eventually but didn't want to leave it in the truck or outside.

Wyatt helped him and then left for the night. Flynn got busy disconnecting and removing the old unit. It was time-consuming and tedious work, but he didn't mind it. He loved electrical work. There was a satisfaction in connecting things and making them work.

He was back inside, working in the small closet that housed the HVAC system when he heard the front door open. He kept his head down, so she wouldn't recognize him right away.

"While I love that you're fixing my air conditioner, do you think you could maybe not make so much of a mess?" He smiled at her words and slowly stood. Turning, he saw her sharp intake of breath.

"It's not like I've made the only mess in here."

"Flynn." Her voice cracked and just for a second she looked vulnerable. "What are you doing here?"

"Wyatt is my brother and we own this building together."

Her eyes faltered as she tried to take in what he'd said. But as fast as a match lighting, they steadied. "You are the new owner of the building?"

"Technically yes, but Wyatt owns the majority. I went in with him to help him out and so that he'd have someone to fix things when needed."

She scrunched her eyes. "But you don't look alike?"

"We're both adopted."

He saw her face soften. "Both of you?"

"Yeah. Our parents couldn't have kids of their own so they got us."

Silence settled in between them before he cleared his throat and spoke. "I'm trying to get as much done tonight so I can make sure this is finished by tomorrow." He walked back to the closet. "I'm sorry my brother took so long to get back to you. He shuts himself off from the world sometimes making it hard to get in touch."

She seemed to finally relax. "I understand how that is. I do that to Avery all the time." She walked over to her small kitchen. "She hates it, but sometimes I just need to...get away from it all."

He continued to work as he talked. "That's what Wyatt says. When we went in together on this building though, he promised he wouldn't do it anymore. That didn't work out so well."

"Well I don't hold it against him and neither should you." Her voice was getting close and when he turned she was directly behind him holding a glass of water. "Thirsty?"

He swallowed hard. "Yeah. Thanks." He took the glass from her, his fingers brushing hers for just a second. Just that one touch had him on edge and aching to touch her more.

"Um, thanks for getting to this so fast. I could have survived without it, but it will be nice not to have to."

"Avery would have me murdered if she knew I owned this building and let you go with air." That wasn't untrue, but it wasn't the reason he was there on a Sunday night.

It was her.

He handed her back his half-empty glass of water. "Speaking of which, I should get back."

"Oh yeah, I'll try to stay out of your way."

"There's no need. I can talk and work at the same time." He turned back to the closet. "Multitasking is one of my best qualities."

She was silent and when he turned his head to look at her, she looked like a deer caught in headlights. "Is everything okay?"

She shook her head and rubbed the back of her hand across her forehead. "Yeah, I'm fine. Just tired."

"I'd like to get about two more hours of work in, then I will be out of your hair."

She waved a hand in the air. "Sure, I'm just going to go into my room and relax."

He didn't say anything as he watched her walk into a room and close the door behind her. She'd been fine for a few minutes, offering him water and a little small talk. She'd been friendly. And then she wasn't. It was like a complete one-eighty.

And fuck if that wasn't part of what turned him on with her.

He loved that she wasn't just nice because that was the thing to do. She let her emotions show, and that was rare. Most people hide behind masks, but not Joy.

No, not Joy. She was who she was and didn't care what people thought.

He didn't see her again that night, so when he went to leave, he knocked on her bedroom door. When she didn't answer, he wasn't sure what to do. On a whim, he cracked open the door and found her asleep, sprawled across her bed.

For minutes he stood and stared at her. She was beautiful all the time, but in sleep, she was gorgeous and peaceful. It was as if all the stress of her life was gone and there was nothing but dreams.

He wanted badly to go to her, hold her and tell her that life could always be how it was in sleep, but he couldn't. They were nothing to each other, at least not yet. But, he was going to change that, and soon.

He wasn't sure why it was her. Why she was the person he wanted? But, he wasn't going to question it.

He was going to embrace it.

Chapter 5

Joy had never wanted a day to end so fast in her life.

When she'd woken up to realize it was morning and that she'd missed saying goodbye to Flynn, she'd thrown a pillow across the room. She hadn't meant to fall asleep, but several days of exhaustion and her dealings with Flynn had knocked her out.

When she'd come home to find him in her apartment, she hadn't been sure what to think. She still wasn't.

He and Wyatt were brothers.

Wyatt, the new building owner. The hot new building owner. Not as hot as Flynn, but still pretty easy on the eyes.

She'd been friendly to Flynn, and it had been easy, until he'd said he was a multi-tasker.

Then she'd had one of her stupid memories of him saying the same thing and she'd shut down.

She'd seen him so clearly. Him telling her that he was great at multitasking with a raise of his eyebrow, like he was suggesting something sexual. Only his face was the only thing that was clear. She couldn't make out any of the surrounding areas or things.

There was no way this was just her imagination running wild. They'd talked before and about a lot of topics.

Which was why, after her first two clients, she was meeting Julia in the park to talk. She needed to get to the bottom of this and fast, because each day, it was getting more and more difficult to stay away from him. But, if they'd already slept together, she might have a lot of explaining to do to him.

Her morning moved fast and soon she was on her way to a small park near the hospital. Julia was already there, eating a salad out of Tupperware.

"Did Wes make that," she said, as she sat down, "because I don't know how he does it, but he makes the best salads."

"He did," she said, "and because we both like you, he made you one too." She pulled another container from her bag.

"Oh God, you guys are the best."

"We know." She smiled as she took another bite.

Opening her own salad, she poured on the side of dressing that was also inside before taking a bite. After she chewed she said, "Flynn was at my place last night."

Fork halfway to her mouth, Julia stopped. "I'm going to need more."

"Apparently, he owns my building along with his brother, Wyatt."

"Is the brother as hot as Flynn?"

Joy rolled her eyes. "Yes, but they are not blood-related. They're both adopted."

"He told you that?"

"Yeah." And she'd remembered it as soon as he'd said it.

"That's kind of a big piece of info for someone to just blurt out."

"When he said Wyatt was his brother, I made the comment that they didn't look alike and that's when he told me they were both adopted. I don't think it's a state secret. Or, at least he didn't make it out to be."

"I take it he was there to fix your air conditioning?"

"Yeah. Wyatt put up more money since Flynn will be doing the repairs and stuff."

Julia's eyes widened. "You guys must have really talked?"

"Not really, that's pretty much it, other than the memory."

"And what was the memory?"

"Him telling me he's great at multitasking with a little twinkle in his eye, like it was a sexual innuendo."

"I bet he is good at multitasking."

"Can we please stay on track here?"

"Sorry." She shrugged and took another bite of her salad.

"Maybe I did sleep with him?"

"And maybe you guys just talked. Tell me more about these memories and be specific."

She told her all the ones she'd had, including yesterday's. Saying each one reminded her how much she seemed to know about him. And that scared her, because if she knew that much about him, did that mean he knew a lot about her? Had she told him things that she never told anyone?

"Those are interesting facts. Things you usually learn on dates. Hometown, first job, pets. Those are not things you talk about during a one-night stand. At least, not any one-night stand I ever had."

She smiled. "Someday I'd like to hear about your one-night stands, but for now, are you saying I didn't sleep with him?"

"I mean, I can't be sure because, you know, I wasn't there, but it really doesn't seem like it."

She sighed in relief. When she slept with him, she fucking wanted to remember it. Wait, had she just thought *when,* like it was a foregone conclusion?

Damn him and his hot body, sexy beard, and intelligent mind.

"Your eyes just went all glassy. Am I to assume you are thinking about sex with the hot lumberjack?"

"I don't want to be, but damn him and his swagger. What is it about him? Seriously? I need to know."

"Have you ever thought that you've been missing something with all the hookups? A connection that you just can't get with sex?"

She dipped her chin and shook her head. "I know that's why I did it. I didn't want connections or conversation."

"Why do you think that was?"

"I don't know." She shrugged. "I just wanted to not have to think."

"And why is that? What didn't you want to think about?"

"Everything." She set her empty bowl down. "My life was a mess. I had nothing. Nobody."

"Tell me about your family? Your parents?"

She never talked about her parents, but something in her wanted to open up. "My dad died when I was five."

"How'd he die?"

"Heart attack. He was older than my mom and died at the age of fifty."

"Did you have a good relationship with him?"

She shook her head. "I don't really remember much about him. He wasn't around a lot, and when he was, he didn't pay too much attention to me or Avery."

"How did you feel when he died?"

She rubbed her lips together and held back tears that were trying to threaten their way through. "I was sad. It didn't matter to me that he hadn't played with me or hung out with me, I still missed him. All mom did was bitch about how he left her high and dry. She never said anything good about him."

"What do you mean left her high and dry?"

"He'd had a lot of debt and left us with virtually nothing. Mom was angry at that and never got over it."

"What happened after that, after his death?"

"I just kinda recoiled and started hiding in my room a lot. Avery hated it because where we used to play together all the time, now I wanted nothing to do with her. I just couldn't be happy anymore."

"Did you blame her for something?"

"No, I was just mad that both she and mom didn't seem to care that he was gone. It was like one day he was there and the next he wasn't, but to them, nothing had changed."

"And you missed your dad?"

She nodded as a lone tear fell down her cheek. She remembered all those years that she'd felt so alone. She never understood how her mom and sister had just gotten over the death so easily. It didn't matter that he'd never been around. He was her dad, and then one day he was gone.

Julia patted her leg. "I think this is a good place to stop. You're holding a lot in, Joy, and have been for some time. I hope talking can help let some of the pain go."

She swallowed the lump that had formed in her throat. "I've avoided it for so long. I'm not sure if it'll do any good, but I'm willing to try." Maybe it was because she was ready to be happy, or maybe it was because she was sick of holding onto it, but either way, she was ready to let go of the past.

"Sometimes just talking things out helps. You may never know why things happened or why you acted the way you did, but hopefully, you will at least come out the other side a little lighter."

"I can see why you chose this field. You're easy to talk to and that makes you good at your job."

She smiled. "There are days, just like everyone else, that I feel useless and that maybe I chose the wrong line of work. But, most of the time, I just like making people smile."

"When should we meet again?"

"I think a week is good. It'll give you time to think about the things you said and dissect them. I'll check my schedule and get back to you."

They parted ways and Joy made her way back to the salon she was currently working at. She had a few more appointments before she'd be done for the day and before she could see Flynn.

She couldn't remember the last time she'd looked forward to seeing someone so much.

It was crazy and rash and every bit of insane as it felt, but none of that seemed to matter to her heart or head. She tried to tell herself that it was just her girl parts that wanted to see him, and that wanting to see him was just sexual, but that hadn't worked.

She couldn't seem to lie to herself.

Only, when she walked into her apartment, he was gone. There was no sign of him anywhere, or that he'd ever even been there. The place was spotless. Not a spec of debris or dust could be seen.

How could he not be there?

She'd gotten herself all worked up to talk to him and he didn't even have the decency to be there. Heart pounding, she paced the small living area, too agitated to do anything else. On one of her turns toward the kitchen, she spotted something on the counter. Upon closer inspection, it was a note.

Joy,

You should be all set. I turned it on so the place would be cool when you got home, but you might want to reset the thermostat to how you like it. If you have any problems, you can go directly through me instead of bothering Wyatt.

Flynn.

He'd left his number and before she had time to change her mind, she pulled her phone from her pocket and sent him a text.

Joy:

You finished fast. I assumed you'd still be here when I got home.

She didn't sign it, instead she figured she'd let him figure out it was her who was texting. As she watched her screen, he texted back.

Flynn:

I figured you'd be glad to have me out of your hair.

Joy:

I am. Kinda.

If she was going in, she might as well dive straight into the deep end.

Joy:

Before Avery and Dax got together, did we ever meet?

She waited and waited and waited. Nothing. A full five minutes went by and she was about ready to text again when her phone vibrated in her hand at the same time that a knock sounded on her door.

Looking down she saw it was Flynn.

Flynn:

Let me in.

She looked up as another knock sounded.

He was there. He came back. God, could she have this conversation in person?

Taking a tentative step toward her door, she steadied herself.

After one last deep breath, she turned the knob and opened the door.

Flynn stood on the other side, dirty, sweaty, and holy cow, sexy. "Um, hey." How lame did she sound?

"Can I come in?"

A quick nod gave him permission before she moved out of the way.

"Sorry I'm so dirty, but after I left here, I worked a couple of hours at another job, and well, when you texted I was around the corner and thought this would be easier." He looked down at himself. "Maybe I should have gone home first."

She swallowed and shook her head. "It's fine." More than fine really. Who knew that dirt could be sexy? She definitely needed to get out more. "Do you want something to drink or to sit down?"

"I wouldn't say no to a beer if you have one, but I probably shouldn't sit."

Without speaking she went to her refrigerator and pulled out two cans of a local brew. She'd started liking them a few months ago, and as she handed him his can, a memory of him saying it was his favorite flashed inside her head like a movie trailer.

Well hell. She'd started drinking this beer because it was his favorite.

"Thanks. You like Lift too? This is my favorite." He popped the top and she watched as he took a long gulp.

"Yeah, I know it is."

His eyes narrowed as he pulled the can from his lips. "You know?"

Setting her own can on the counter behind her, she rubbed a hand over her forehead. "Just tell me this...did we have sex?"

He studied her quizzically for a few seconds. "You really don't remember?"

"Oh God, we did, didn't we?" She turned and started pacing again.

"Joy stop." She froze in her tracks at his voice. "Look at me." She turned to face him again. "We didn't have sex."

"We didn't? Then how do I know all these crazy things about you, like your favorite fucking beer, which is now my favorite, or that you had a brother who was adopted, or that you're from Indianapolis, and instead of going to college like your parents wanted, you went to a technical school to learn electrical work because it fascinated you. Your favorite fucking color is yellow because it reminds you of your mom, and you hate hot dogs because they creep you out. How in the hell do I know all this stuff?"

He was smiling like a lunatic. "Because I told you."

"But when?"

"I can't believe you remember all that, and by the way, my favorite color used to be yellow. Now it's pale blue."

She pursed her lips and put her hands on her hips. "How do I know all this?"

"Months ago, at the end of December, we met. The place was pretty empty because it was a weeknight, and you hit on me. I turned you down, but not before making some stupid joke that made you laugh, and then somehow, you sat down and we spent the next couple hours together talking."

"I hit on you and you turned me down." She groaned. "That's twice now that I've hit on you and twice you've turned me down. Am I that hideous?" It was completely off subject, but she was just vain enough to want to know.

His eyes softened. "You are not hideous at all. On the contrary. But that night, well it had been a shitty day for me. And, as hot as you were, I wasn't in the mood for what you were offering. And the second time, when Dax was there, well I was kinda pissed that you didn't recognize me. Sure, I knew I didn't have the beard, but that you had the balls to hit on me and two of my friends, like I never even existed, hurt."

All the tension went out of her body. "I don't know why I can't remember that night. Can you tell me about it? Maybe it will jog my memory."

He took another long sip of his beer before speaking. "After you sat down, we just started talking. About everything. You told me about Avery, and about your dad dying, and then later on your mom. I told you how I was adopted because my parents couldn't have kids. We talked about our jobs and our childhoods. Movies, music and books. Anything and everything you can think of, we talked about. I thought we were hitting it off and I was planning on asking for your number. But then you left."

"What do you mean I left?" She knew deep down that she wasn't going to like this.

"One second we were laughing, and the next you abruptly said you had to go to the bathroom, and you never came back."

She dropped her head back and closed her eyes as it all came rushing back. Their conversations, the fun, and laughter. His face as his eyes lit up and that fucking beard. And then the fear. The fear that she was letting him in, that maybe, she could actually like him.

So she ran.

That was her way.

When something scared her, she bolted.

Opening her eyes, she stared into his. She owed him the truth. "I remember now. I left because you scared me."

"I scared you?" He looked panicked. "If I said or did anything that wasn't appropriate or that was out of line, I'm sorry."

"It wasn't that. You scared me because I was having fun and I liked you. That was not something I was used to." She shook her head. "It's not an excuse, but I was going through a lot, and honestly, I was a pretty shitty person back then and for a long time before."

He shook his head, a smile turning up the corner of his mouth. "I still can't believe you didn't remember. All these months I've been staring a hole through you wondering why the hell you were ignoring me. We had so much fun that night just talking. It was like the best date I'd ever been on, even though it wasn't a date."

"All those times you were staring at me, I was having crazy thoughts, which I now know are memories about you. I thought I was going insane because they would only happen when you were around or if someone brought up your name."

"That's why you thought we'd had sex?"

"Yeah, kinda. They were normal things at first like movies and music, but one day I remembered the feel of your skin and figured we must have...you know." She looked down at the floor.

"My beard," he said, a half-smile on his face.

"What about your beard?" God she loved that fucking beard.

"You touched it that night and when you did your fingers grazed my skin."

Their eyes met and the air between them sizzled. Her fingers twitched at the memory of his skin, and all she wanted to do was touch him again. Any part of him would do, but God, she wished it was lips on lips.

He took a step closer watching as he set his beer can on the counter next to hers. He was maybe two feet from her now and her heart was beating so fast she was sure he could hear it.

"I only had the beard that night because I'd been too lazy to shave after the whole No Shave November thing the guys at work did. But after you left me, I didn't want it anymore. I wanted no reminder of that night. Until that night with Dax. When you didn't recognize me, I swore it was the beard, so I grew it back out."

She ran her eyes down and over the beard. "It's longer now."

He moved another step closer making her have to tilt her neck, even more, to look up at him. "You said you liked it."

"I do." Without meaning to, she lifted a hand and gently ran her fingers over it. His eyes never wavered, never left hers, but they did flare with even more heat.

"Is the fear gone?"

It took a second, but she finally understood what he was asking. "I'm still afraid, but I'm learning how to deal with the fear now." She dropped her hand from his beard.

"And this," he reached out a hand, lightly placing it on her hip, "is what you want?"

She bit her bottom lip and looked between them to where he was touching her. Just that one little touch, lit her on fire. But,oh God, why did there have to be a but. She promised herself she wouldn't take sex lightly anymore. That she wouldn't be the person she used to be.

"I don't know," she answered honestly.

Immediately his hand dropped from her hip and she instantly missed it. She could tell he was fighting an internal battle with himself, so she put him out of his misery.

"I know this is going to sound like a line, but it's not you, it's me. I promised myself that I was going to be a better person. That I would never again use sex as a way to hide from my life or my problems." She shook her head and gave a little chuckle. "Although, right this minute, I'm seriously wondering if I should just say fuck being a better person."

His smile put her at ease. "While I think you don't give yourself enough credit for how good of a person you are, I don't want to be the reason you go back on something you want." He again lifted his hand only this time he ran one finger down her cheek making her shiver. "Why don't we try for friends?"

Just that one touch of his finger to her face and she was tongue-tied. She'd be a bowl of mush when his cock was inside her.

Oh fuck. Why'd she have to think that?

"I can probably do friends." If she didn't die of sexual frustration first.

Taking a step back, he gave her a small wink. "Anything will be better than you ignoring me whenever we're in the same room."

"I wasn't ignoring you, I was saving my sanity." She also took a step back and sat down on the stool behind her. "The memories were playing havoc with what I thought was reality. It doesn't help that you are so goddamn good looking either."

"I'll try to be more ugly if it'll help." She laughed. She loved his sense of humor. That was something she now remembered from their night together. He'd made her laugh, which was something that until that night, she hadn't done a lot of.

"Try wearing a shirt." Every time he took his off she wanted to hyperventilate. And, because it was Summer in Ohio, she swore she saw him without a shirt more than she did with one.

"Should I wear long sleeves? Maybe a sweatshirt?" He was teasing her and he was still sexy.

This being friends thing was going to be tough.

Especially, when she was in month seven of no sex. How was she supposed to hold out against his hotness when all her body wanted was orgasms? So many orgasms.

And not the ones from her vibrator. Those were fake orgasms. She wanted real ones, from a real man. Although, to be fair, she couldn't recall the last time she'd even had a real one with an actual guy. Those last few times, she'd faked it just to be finished faster.

What kind of person fakes it during a one-night stand?

The kind of person who was afraid and lonely and was just looking for some kind of human contact.

"I think I should go," he said, making her look up at him. "It's been a long day."

"Oh yeah, I didn't mean to make it longer."

His head shook slightly and laughed. "This might have been the best part of my day."

She raised her eyebrows. "You are a sick man, Flynn." His smile grew even bigger.

"See ya soon?" He said it as a question.

"Yeah, I think so."

He walked out of her apartment, and when she shut the door behind him, she dropped back against it.

She was going to be friends with Flynn.

Hot, lumberjack, bearded Flynn.

What had she gotten herself into?

Chapter 6

She'd said his name.

His name had come out of her mouth. Off of her lips.

He'd replayed her saying it over and over again for hours. Even when his head hit his pillow, that was all he could think about.

That was the first time in the seven months, since he'd first met her, that she'd said his name, and it had twisted things up inside him.

When he'd gotten the first text from her, his fucking heart had actually faltered in his chest. She'd contacted him. That was huge. But, then when she asked if they'd met before, it practically stopped. She hadn't been ignoring him. She didn't remember. He'd been on his way home, and ironically, he was right around the corner from her apartment.

The timing couldn't have been more perfect.

And now, here he was trying to sleep, his cock as hard as it had ever been, all because she'd said his name.

Closing his eyes, he replayed their conversation for the four-hundredth time. He was still so shocked that she hadn't remembered him and their night together.

That night was one of the best of his life, and somehow, for some reason, she had blocked it out.

He understood fear, knew that it was different for each person, but to fear having fun? That was definitely a new one.

From what he knew of her, which was only stuff he'd learned from Dax or Avery, she had been in a downward spiral since her mom had died, right after Joy and Avery had finished high school. That meant for the last five years, she'd been unhappy. More than that, she'd been sad. And that just wouldn't do. Nobody should have to live life sad, especially not someone as vibrant and unique as Joy.

She was gorgeous with her long blond hair and dimples in her cheeks. Though those only showed when she smiled, which wasn't often. But, she was more than her looks. She was funny and smart, and she made him feel good.

That had to mean something, right?

Each and every time he was around her, he felt good. And that feeling—God he wanted to feel it all the time. But, he also wanted her to feel good and to be happy. Only, he had no idea how to go about making that happen for her.

Rolling to his back, he threw an arm over his head and stared up into the skylight in his ceiling.

The skylight was one of the reasons he'd bought this house. As a kid growing up, the sky was the one thing that never changed from foster home to foster home. He didn't recall much about those early years, hell he'd been under five years of age, but he did remember loving the sky. When he'd finally been adopted he spent the first several years getting out of bed in the middle of the night to go outside and look at the sky. Then one day, he came home from school and above his bed, was a skylight. His dad and mom had somehow known. That was the moment he knew he was home, that they were for real, and actually wanted him.

It was the moment he finally relaxed.

He wanted Joy to know what that was like. To finally let down her guard and let it all go, knowing that nothing bad was going to happen.

He wanted to be her home.

And because that thought freaked the fuck out of him, he knew it would do the same to her.

When morning dawned, he rushed through his morning routine so he could get to the office early. He had some paperwork to deal with before heading to a job site.

He loved his job with Dax's company and thanked his lucky stars for the day they'd met. Dax hadn't hesitated to hire him even though he'd been green and lacking in any real references. But, he loved what he did, and because of that, he did it well and that had shown. Now he was a foreman and second in charge, at the age of thirty.

God, had it really been ten years since he'd moved to Cedarville?

He'd left Indiana right after technical school. Not because he hated it there, or wanted to get away from his parents, but because he wanted to make it on his own. Both his mom and dad were respected and well known in the town they'd lived in, and if he had stayed, someone would have offered him a job only because he was their kid. That might have been fine for some people, but not for him.

He wanted to do something by himself. To show the world that he was good enough.

His parents had understood and even encouraged him to go out and find his own way once, again reminding him how lucky he really was.

Arriving at the warehouse which housed the offices, he saw that Dax was already there. No surprise really, since now that he was with Avery, he usually tried to get in early so he could be home with her in the evenings.

He found him in his office, head down as he studied something on his desk.

"Morning." He stood in the doorway.

"Hey." He lifted his head. "You're in early."

"I was up and thought I might as well come in."

"You know, you're starting to sound a lot like me before I met Avery. All work and no play isn't good."

He flipped him off. "I play plenty."

"Yeah, when was the last time you went out after work?"

He stepped into the room, taking a seat in front of the desk. He hated to admit that it had been a while, but going to bars hadn't been high on his list ever since meeting Joy. "It gets old, going to bars every night."

"I know that, but I thought you were the ultimate bachelor and loved being single?"

"I'm not sure where you ever came up with that idea. I'd have no problem settling down. In fact I would prefer it."

Dax studied him, leaning back in his chair. "There's a woman, isn't there?"

Damn the fool for knowing him so well. "Maybe. I'm not sure yet." He wasn't ready to tell his friend that it was, in fact, his soon to be sister-in-law who was the star of all his fantasies.

"When you're ready to talk, I'm here to listen. You listened to me babble on about Avery, so the least I can do is return the favor."

He nodded. "Once I figure out what's happening, I'll take you up on that." He studied the carpet on the floor for a second. "Do you ever wonder why some people can go through trauma and come out the other side fine and others never get over it?"

He sat forward and braced his arms on his desk. "I don't think I've ever really thought about it, but if I had to guess, I'd say that we all deal with things differently. Where one person might be able to work through it and let it go, another can't. Take Avery and Joy for example."

Flynn sat up straighter in his seat at Joy's name. "What about them?" He was going to get information without even mentioning to Dax that she was the woman.

"Joy never got over the death of her dad when she was five, and then, when it happened again with her mom, it got even worse. Avery says she was almost a recluse after their dad died, but after their mom passed, she turned to using sex as a way of comfort. But Avery, somehow she was able to find a way out from the pain and move on with her life."

"Is Joy still that way?" He hoped his voice sounded calm and relaxed and not frantic, which was how he felt inside. He'd suspected – from the two times she'd tried to pick him up – that sex was her method of dealing with her pain. But suspecting and hearing it were two different things.

"She's been better the last several months. Avery says she hasn't been to a bar for the purpose of picking up a guy since before she got attacked. And from what she told Avery, she hasn't had sex since before Christmas."

That made him perk up. They'd met right after Christmas. Could there be some kind of correlation between the two? Had she unconsciously stopped sleeping around because of him?

He sure had. While he hadn't been going out every night picking up women to sleep with, he had done that. He'd even had a few regulars he could call when all he wanted was sex. But that all stopped after he met her. He hadn't been with anyone since before Thanksgiving.

And his body was well aware.

"Speaking of Joy," Dax said. "Was that her air conditioning you fixed yesterday?"

"Yeah, remember when I went in on the building a couple of months ago with Wyatt? Turns out it's the building where Joy lives."

"How did you not know that since until recently, Wes lived there too?"

He shrugged. "It's not like Wes ever mentioned the exact building he lived in. There are like ten apartment buildings in that area. The only time I ever went there was to check it out before buying it."

"I take it you got her all squared away?"

"Yep, she's all set." In more ways than one, he hoped. He stood. "I hope you're taking some time off this week before the wedding?"

"Friday and then all next week. I'm surprising Avery with a trip to Mexico."

"She's a lucky woman."

"I'm the lucky one."

He wanted that. He wanted to feel like the luckiest bastard in the world because a woman loved him. To know that he would do anything for a woman just because he loved her.

He had a sneaking suspicion that Joy was that woman, but he needed to take his time and not rush her. She was not a woman who could be rushed, especially when it came to love and relationships.

Only his own heart was having a hard time understanding that. It wanted to leap and deal with consequences later.

Not a good idea.

After an hour in his office doing paperwork, he loaded up his work truck and hit one of the job sites. The company had five jobs going at the moment, and he'd been flipping between them for the last week. But today, he was needed for some electrical at the remodel of a doctor's office complex.

He had four other guys on site with him and together they worked fast and efficiently. Because he wanted to finish the electrical work in one day, he worked straight through lunch, only eating a granola bar.

At ten after six, he finally finished. Since he let his guys go at five, he was the last one there. As he loaded up his truck, his stomach rumbled, making him realize how hungry he was. After a quick stop at the warehouse where he traded out his work truck for his own truck, he headed straight to Dockside for a meal.

The place was pretty busy for a Tuesday, and he hoped he'd be able to find a seat at the bar. Sure enough, there was one seat open at the end.

"Hey Flynn," Sabrina, the bartender said in greeting, dropping a napkin down in front of him. "What'll you have?"

"A Lift please. Is Wes working today?" He knew he had hired a new cook to help out so now he was never sure when he was around.

"Yep. I'll tell him you're here."

She slid the full pint of beer down in front of him and he picked it up, taking a long drink. As he was sitting it down, he heard a laugh that had him immediately turning.

Joy.

She was walking in with Julia by her side. Her blonde hair was pulled up into a high ponytail and she was dressed in black capri pants and a blouse type shirt.

As always, she was gorgeous.

She hadn't spotted him yet, but she turned toward the bar while Julia kept walking toward the kitchen. The moment she noticed him, she stopped walking. He nodded, indicating that he saw her, and she began moving again.

"You want my seat?" he asked since the bar was full.

Shaking her head, she moved to stand on the right of him. There was just enough space for her to stand, but only if she brushed her side up against his. Which she did.

He worked hard not to moan out loud.

But in his head...there was lots of moaning going on.

"I don't mind standing. I sat most of the day." She waved to Sabrina who waved back and indicated she'd be right with her. "You just get here or are you finished?"

"Just got here." He passed her his beer. "Drink?"

She eyed it for a second before wrapping her fingers around the glass, hers brushing his, and taking it out of his hand. He watched as she tipped her head back and took a long sip.

His cock hardened in his pants as she swallowed it down. Shifting in his seat, he turned his body slightly away from her.

"Thanks," she said and set the glass back on the bar. "I needed that."

"Long day?" He was surprised he could speak considering all the blood in his body was currently below his waist.

"Not so much long, as annoying. One of the regular nail techs called out and I had to cover for her."

"Does that happen a lot?" He had no clue how being a nail tech worked. He knew she was only a contractor and didn't actually work at one salon. That was all the knowledge he had.

"Not usually." She leaned one elbow on the bar and turned to the side, facing him. "And, if it does, I don't generally get stuck with the clients. It's part of my deal with the salons. But I was feeling generous today. I blame you for that. So, I volunteered."

"Me? What did I do?"

She raised a perfectly sculpted eyebrow. "You made me remember." She smiled, and in that moment, he wondered why he ever questioned that she was the one.

She was absolutely, positively, the woman for him.

"I'm sorry to have caused you so much trouble," he joked.

Sabrina chose that moment to slide a pint in front of Joy apparently knowing her drink of choice. "Either of you eating?"

"Can I get the jambalaya," he said.

"Same," Joy said, giving him a sideways glance.

"Coming up."

"Do you always get the jambalaya?" she asked.

"It's my favorite, so maybe half the time."

She nodded.

"What about you?"

"It's my favorite too." She said it quietly, her eyes holding his gaze.

He leaned in a little closer to her. "I'm sure a lot of people order it." He wanted to put her at ease so she wouldn't run.

Her eyes searched his, and he hoped they held humor, instead of the lust he actually felt.

"You're probably right." She lifted her beer to her lips and took a small sip. "How was your day?" she asked, setting the glass back down.

"Busy, but that's nothing new. I'm trying to stay ahead of schedule since Dax will be gone next week." As soon as the words were out, he remembered that the honeymoon was a secret. He hoped she would just ignore it, or maybe, that she hadn't totally been paying attention.

"Why won't Dax be at work next week?" No such luck.

He sighed and moved a little closer to her, whispering, "You can't tell Avery, but Dax is taking her on a honeymoon."

A slow smile appeared on her face. "Of course he is." She shook her head and let out a little laugh. "He really would do anything for her."

"Isn't that how it's supposed to be? When you are in love?"

She shrugged and averted her eyes from him, looking down at her beer. "The only knowledge I have of love is from movies."

"Don't you think movies are based in some sort of reality? I do, or at least, I hope they are, otherwise, what's it all for?"

Her head turned until she was looking at him again. "You are a constant surprise to me."

"I don't know why." He lifted his arms in a small shrug. "I've never tried to be anything other than myself."

"I'm starting to see that. Not everyone is, you know."

"It's too hard to pretend to be someone you're not. Or, at least I assume it is."

Sabrina walked over then, sliding both their bowls of jambalaya onto the bar. "Enjoy!" As quickly as she'd appeared, she was gone.

Flynn looked over to her as she opened her napkin. "Any suggestions on something I can get Avery and Dax for a wedding gift? Dax said not to get them anything, but my mom raised me better than that."

"Oh God, don't remind me. I've been thinking for three days and still haven't come up with anything."

"It's easier when people register, that's for sure."

They ate in silence for a few minutes until she said, "What about something personalized, like a rug or door sign?"

"That's a good idea, you should do that."

"I mean, you could get them that, if you wanted."

Smiling, he took another bite. "I will come up with something, you should do that though. It's perfect."

"I'm not sure if I'll be able to have it made in time? So maybe it's not a good idea."

"You don't have to have it for the wedding. Just as long as it's finished by the time they get back."

Her eyes lit up. "Oh good point."

Flynn took another bite and then saw Wes walking toward them out of the corner of his eyes.

"Hey, two of my favorite people." He slapped Flynn on the back and pulled Joy's ponytail. "Did you guys come together or is this just a happy coincidence?"

"I came with your wife, I assumed you knew that?" Joy gave him a look that made Flynn laugh.

"I was too busy saying hi to her to ask any questions." He shrugged, like he wasn't talking about making out with his wife, when they both knew he was.

"Can you maybe stop groping each other near the food? Or, at least don't tell me about it. Some of us like to at least pretend the food we are eating is clean.

"I love you, Joy, but you have got to loosen up."

She scoffed at him. "I'm as loose as they come."

Flynn choked at her words. "Um you might want to rethink those words."

This time he was on the receiving end of one of her looks. "You both knew what I meant."

"I gotta get back, I just wanted to come out and say hello."

They said goodbye as Wes walked back to the kitchen.

"How do you like living alone now that Wes is gone?"

"I don't really mind living alone. It was just nice to have a roommate so that I could save some money."

"Isn't that a two-bedroom? There are probably one-bedrooms that are less expensive?"

"I liked the owner the best at this place, although, now that I think about it, that's not even a reason anymore since you are the owner."

"First, Wyatt is the owner, and second, did you just say you didn't like me?" He was smiling and trying to hold in a laugh.

"Wyatt, I forgot about him. He was pretty nice and cute. Really cute." She was goading him, he could tell.

"Stay away from my brother." He said it with no authority or emotion even though he wanted to demand that she listen to him.

"Afraid I'll chew him up and spit him out?"

He rubbed his lips together and wondered if he should say what he was thinking. He might as well. "More afraid you'll like him better than me."

Her eyes widened and, for a second, he thought he saw interest and maybe heat.

God, he hoped it was heat.

"You know I like you," she said, her voice barely a whisper.

"Enough to go on a date with me?"

The bar was busy and loud and there were people everywhere, but to Flynn, it was just him and Joy. He saw only her and his heart beat steadily in his chest while he waited for her answer.

And then, she did what she always did, made him laugh. "Can I phone a friend?"

"What?"

"You know, like the game show. I need help so I want to phone a friend."

"You need help deciding whether or not you want to go out on a date with me?" For a second he wondered if he was dreaming. But then he remembered that, in his dreams, he and Joy rarely, if ever, spoke.

It was all sex, all the time.

She blew out a breath. "You confuse me and I'm not good with confusion."

He leaned sideways, his elbow on the bar. "Who would you ask?"

"Maybe Wes or Julia."

"You know, they both just happen to be in this very building."

She bit her lip again, something he was getting very used to seeing. "Would it be okay if I went and talked to them?"

He gestured with his arm. "Be my guest."

She scurried away and he watched her go. He had no idea what was happening. With Joy, it seemed that every second was an adventure. But he didn't mind. She kept him on his toes and he liked it.

More than liked it.

Wished, in fact, that she'd do it more often.

Now he just had to wait and find out her answer.

Chapter 7

Pushing open the swinging door that led to the kitchen, she found both Wes and Julia staring at her.

"Help me."

"Are you dying?" Wes said casually, "because you look fine to me."

"Jackass." She turned to Julia. "Flynn just asked me out. What do I do?"

"For starters, you don't leave him out there to come back here and get our advice. It's like you're twelve and have never dated before."

"I haven't dated before!" she practically shouted.

"I have so many questions that I don't know where to start."

"There's no time for that. We can deal with all my neurosis the next time you poke at my mind, but right now I need an answer."

"Do you like him?" Wes asked.

She wasn't sure how to answer that. So she went with honesty. "Does wanting to lick every inch of his body count?"

"Yes," they both said at the same time.

She opened her mouth to speak, but then shut it. Was attraction a good enough reason to date someone?

"Like Julia," Wes said, "I have a ton of questions starting with, since when have you wanted to lick Flynn's whole body? But we can let that go for now. You obviously find him attractive, so why not say yes to a date?"

"What if I date him, we end up in bed together, and then, just like all the other guys I've slept with, that's it?"

"This isn't a whim," Julia said. "You've thought about this for months, so it's not going to end that way. Plus, I have a feeling that Flynn won't let it."

Wes looked at Julia. "You knew about this and didn't tell me?"

"Doctor-patient confidentiality."

He frowned. "I'm not sure I like this new arrangement you two have."

"Deal with it," Joy said, still wondering if Julia was right. Was it different with Flynn?

"Stop thinking about it," Julia said as she turned her around and pushed her toward the door. "This is not you being flippant. This is a nice guy who you know and like. And, if it matters so much to you, maybe try not sleeping with him on the first date."

She lifted her own hands to brace against the door. Without turning around she said, "That is not a promise I can make," and pushed out into the restaurant. With all the confidence she could muster, she walked over to where Flynn was still sitting at the bar.

As she moved up to stand beside him, he turned his head, a mocking grin on his face. He didn't speak, only continued to stare at her.

"Yes," she said, nodding. "I will go on a date with you."

His eyes flared, and for a second, it seemed as if he was going to lean in and kiss her.

God, she wanted that more than anything.

And that had her leaning away from him.

She couldn't trust her feelings, at least when it came to anything sex-related. She was going to do this right and take it nice and slow.

"That's fantastic." He pushed his stool back, pulling his wallet from his back pocket. He threw several bills on the bar and picked up his beer, downing the last of it. "Now that our first date is over, I look forward to our next one."

"What are you talking about?"

"We just had our first date."

"No we didn't. We happened to be eating a meal at the same place."

He shrugged. "Maybe that's how you see it, but I see it as a date. We shared a beer and I paid. If that's not a date, then I don't know what is." He turned as if to walk away, and then at the last second, turned only his head to face her. "Now that the first date's out of the way, I figure maybe getting you to agree to a second one will be a lot easier." With that, he walked away, leaving her to do nothing but stand and watch him go.

What the fuck had just happened?

Long after he'd walked out the door, she continued to stand there. It wasn't until she heard Sabrina say her name that she turned back to the bar and sat in the seat that Flynn had vacated.

"You okay?" Sabrina asked.

She laughed because it was that or cry and she didn't cry. "That fucking man is insane."

"Flynn? Seems like a pretty normal guy to me."

"It's always the normal ones who crack first." She lifted her glass to her mouth and took a sip of her beer. She watched as Sabrina picked up the money Flynn had thrown on the bar.

"Man leaves a tip like this can't be all that bad."

Joy continued to drink, lifting her free hand to flip Sabrina off. She wanted someone to be on her side. Someone to agree that the man was crazy.

When her beer was gone, she pushed the glass to the back of the bar and sighed. Sabrina had moved on to help someone else, so it was just her and her thoughts.

All of which happened to be about Flynn.

"So," Julia said, coming to stand in front of her behind the bar. "What happened?"

"Since you're back there, be useful and get me another beer."

Julia glared at her for about twenty seconds, then went and poured her a beer. She didn't work there, but since her husband was the owner, she pretty much did whatever she wanted. And because Wes loved her, he let her.

"Now spill," she said when she set the beer down in front of her.

"Apparently, according to Flynn, this was our first date." She lifted the glass and took a drink.

"Explain please?"

"When I came back out, I told him that, yes, I would go on a date with him. He then said, good because we just had our first date. He threw some money on the bar and left."

Julia leaned on the bar. "Oh, he's good."

She practically growled. "What the hell does that mean?"

"He knew you were hesitant about dating him so he pulled a fast one on you by paying for your meal. Now you've been on a date."

She dropped her head on the bar. "Is all dating this confusing and frustrating?"

"Only when you like the person. If you didn't like him, there would be nothing to be confused or frustrated about."

Lifting her head, she took another sip of her beer. "This is why I've avoided it for so long."

"I don't think that's true. I think you thought you were avoiding it, but in reality, no one ever piqued your interest enough that you wanted to date them."

Pursing her lips, she thought about that. She'd found some guys interesting and some guys cute or sexy, but there was no one who made her stop and catch her breath or smile just thinking of his name. Or hell, come twice a night when she got herself off.

Just Flynn.

Sexy, smart, funny, annoying, frustrating Flynn.

"So what do I do?"

"That depends, do you still want to go out with him?"

That was easy. "Yes."

"My suggestion is that you don't wait too long to call him and ask him out."

"I have to ask him out?" No, that was not what she wanted to do.

"This is the twenty-first century, Joy. Women are allowed to make the first move."

She bit her lip. It wasn't that she was afraid to make the first move, it's that she'd done that a lot with all the guys she'd picked up in bars. She didn't want Flynn to be just another guy. "I know all about making the first move I just..." She dropped her head back and took a deep breath. "I've done that, but this feels different."

Julia nodded and drummed her fingers on the bar. "Okay, I think I get it now. What if you didn't ask him out, but instead you initiated a conversation with him? Like you text him or maybe you happen to run into him somewhere?"

"I could probably do that. At least the texting one. I don't know where he hangs out."

"He eats here several times a week and, since you know the owner, you just might be able to get him to text you when he's here."

"Is this what you tell your patients to do? Stalk people?"

"It's not stalking, you fool. It's using your friends to make sure you are in the right place at the right time."

"I'll be sure to tell the police that when I get arrested."

"Seriously though, I think this will work. You'll get to see and talk to him which will help you guys get to know each other."

She felt like she already knew a ton about him from that night back in December, but she'd like to know more. But, that scared her, because if she wanted to get to know him, then surely she would have to tell him about herself. And, that was not a subject she liked to talk about.

"I'm gonna get out of here," she said, pushing her chair back and standing up. It had been a long day, and she was ready to relax with her feet up.

"Keep me in the loop."

Joy waved goodbye and walked out the front door to her car. The short drive home her mind stayed on Flynn. On how good he'd looked, how nice he'd been, and how his eyes were always watching her.

She knew, because she couldn't stop looking at him.

Which led to her imagining him naked.

On her bed.

Or, maybe the floor.

Or hell, the counter right there in the bar.

She was utterly fucked.

In her apartment, which was nice and cool thanks to Flynn, she tried everything to stop thinking about him. She took a shower, did her dishes, and even, fucking vacuumed.

Nothing worked.

Flopping down onto her couch, phone in hand, she pulled up her text thread with him. For more than five minutes she just stared at his name at the top. When her eyes started to blur, she sighed and gave in to texting him.

Joy:

What was that bullshit you pulled earlier?

She never took her eyes off her phone while she waited for his response. Only ten minutes later she was still waiting. It didn't even show that he'd read it. What could he be doing? When he left Dockside, had he gone somewhere else?

Leaving her phone on the couch, she stood up and walked out onto her small patio. Her view wasn't anything great, just the woods, but she always felt calm when she was out there. When she heard a noise, she looked to her left and saw her neighbor, Norah on her own patio.

"Looks like we had the same idea," she said, loud enough so that Norah could hear her.

"It's so peaceful out here. And tonight it's not that hot." She turned to face Joy. "Did you get your air fixed?"

"I did. Although, with today's weather, I probably would have been fine without it."

"I saw someone come and go yesterday so I figured that's who it was."

"That was probably Flynn." And there she went thinking about him again. "He was the one who fixed it."

"He's not the owner of the building is he?"

"One of them, yes. His brother, Wyatt, is in charge, but Flynn will do any repairs that are needed."

"Sounds like you know him?"

"If being a pain in my ass means I know him, then yeah, I guess I do." A gorgeous pain in her ass, but Norah didn't need to hear about that. "He actually works for my soon to be brother-in-law."

"Small world."

Joy wanted to talk more to Norah, maybe get to the bottom of why she was so reserved, but she heard her phone ding with an incoming text and all she could think about was Flynn.

"Have a good night!" She yelled, as she stepped back inside and pulled the door closed.

She was breathing heavily, not from running, but from thinking it could be Flynn. The message might not even be from Flynn. It could be anyone. She slowed her steps and sat down before picking up her phone. Taking a deep breath she finally lifted it up.

Flynn:

It wasn't bullshit. You were nervous about going out with me, so I solved the problem. And look, now you are texting me.

Joy:

I wasn't nervous.

Flynn:

You're a lot of things Joy but you aren't a liar.

Joy:

How do you know what I am?

Flynn:

I've paid attention.

Joy:

So maybe I was nervous. That doesn't mean you solved anything with your pseudo date. We still have to have a real first one.

Flynn:

Maybe before we do that, we can get to know each other like this.

Joy:

Over text?

Flynn:

If that's easier for you?

Joy:

I guess. Hearing your voice would be better.

Why had she said that? And damn her for hitting send before she could stop herself.

She jumped when her phone rang in her hand.

She'd made her bed, so now it was time to lie in it. Only she wished she were lying in it with him.

Hitting answer, she said, "You know, it's starting to annoy me that you do that."

"Do what?"

"Call me when we are texting."

"Sometimes talking is easier, especially when things can get misconstrued."

She pulled her legs up under her butt and leaned onto the armrest. "Has anyone ever told you that you're a strange guy?"

His laugh went straight to her vagina. "Surprisingly, no. That means that you are one of a kind."

"Oh, that I already knew." She chewed on her bottom lip. "Why me?"

She heard him huff out a breath. "Do you want the whole list, because it's long?"

That made her smile. "No, I'm just trying to understand. I'm not that great."

"For someone so self-assured, you really don't think very highly of yourself, do you?"

"I know who I am, Flynn and it's not a person who guys flock over. Not unless I am drunk and offering sex."

"I..." he paused, and she could hear movement in the background. "Are you trying to piss me off?"

She wasn't sure what he meant. "If it bothers you that I slept around then maybe we shouldn't be talking."

"Fuck that, Joy. I couldn't care less who or how many guys you slept with. What pisses me off is when you put yourself down. You're better than that."

A warm heat spread through her whole body. Hearing him say he didn't care who she'd slept with went a long way to easing her mind. It was how she'd chosen to live her life, even though she'd never been happy or comfortable with it. She wasn't slut-shaming. If a woman wanted to, and was happy with sleeping with different guys, more power to her. It's the knowing what you want and who you are part that is important. And, she'd never had any clue. All she knew was that she was unhappy and wanted to try to find love.

Only love didn't work that way.

"I'm working on it. I've never been very good at knowing who I am."

His voice softened. "I could help with that, you know."

She laughed. "You're a glutton for punishment aren't you?"

"When I see something I like, I go after it. And right now, that's you." He paused. "Is that going to be a problem?"

Was it? Hell she had no clue. But, she wasn't going to ruin it before she had the chance to find out.

"As long as you know that this will probably end badly, I guess I'm in." She yawned, covering it with her hand.

"You're tired, I should let you go."

Panic set in. She wasn't ready to end the conversation. "I'm not that tired." She hoped he took her hint.

"Is that you saying you'd like to keep talking?"

While she was glad he understood, she was also unnerved that he seemed to get her. "Only if you want to?"

"There's nothing else I'd enjoy more. Well, there are a couple of things, but I can wait for those."

She laughed and made herself more comfortable on the couch. "At least one of us can."

This time he laughed. "I didn't say waiting would be easy. While you just remembered our conversation from six months ago, I've been living with it daily. And I gotta say, I'm pretty fucking obsessed with you."

Her breath hitched at his confession. And the way he'd said it, as if it was just a regular statement, like I enjoy hiking, or my favorite food is pickles. Who did that?

"I might not have remembered the whole thing until a couple of days ago, but I did have some memories of you. So don't pretend you're the only one who is obsessed." Her eyes went wide when she realized what she'd said. What was it with her diarrhea of the mouth when she talked to him?

"Um, can you say that again? You're obsessed with me?"

"I have no idea what you are talking about. You must be hearing things."

Again he laughed, only this time it was deep and sultry making her desperately wish she could see his face. "You're killing me, but damn if I can even seem to care right now."

If they were going to keep talking, she needed to change the subject. "Tell me a story?"

"What kind of story?"

"I don't even care. Just something about you." She wanted to know everything there was to know about him. Even the smallest things.

"Where I grew up, we had woods right behind our house. It was great. Wyatt and I would go back there to play and make forts and hideouts. One time, when I was maybe ten, I had to pee so bad and instead of going all the way back to the house, I decided I would just go right there in the woods. I mean, I was a boy, right, and boys could easily pee in the woods. Well, little did I know that there was poison ivy where I decided to do my business."

"Oh no!" She was trying not to laugh but it was nearly impossible.

"Hours later I began itching and couldn't stop. When my mom finally looked, and yes, it was mortifying to have my mom look at my junk at age ten, all she could do was laugh. No joke. She laughed so hard that she had to sit down and my dad had to come help me. It was marginally better to have my dad be the one helping spread anti-itch cream on my penis, but it was still horrible. For years after that, especially when I started dating, my mom used that scenario as a reminder to keep my privates out of places they didn't belong."

By the end of the story she was laughing so hard that tears were rolling down her cheeks.

"I'm glad my story amuses you."

When she could finally catch her breath she said, "I feel like your mom might be my kindred spirit because that is for sure how I would parent."

"Yeah, my mom wasn't one of those moms who would sit down, rub our backs and tell us everything would be okay. Don't get me wrong, she was always there for me and Wyatt, and we both knew how much she loved us, but she wasn't nurturing in a conventional way. She was at every game we had or event we did and she encouraged us whenever we needed it. But, when we did stupid things, she didn't hesitate to tell us or even laugh at us."

His mom sounded amazing. "Sounds like a pretty good childhood."

"I have no complaints, especially since it could have been a lot worse."

"Because you were adopted?" After she said it she wondered if maybe she shouldn't have. Maybe it was a sore subject, or maybe it was too heavy for their first real conversation.

"I know how lucky I am. Had my birth mom not ended up dead, I could have been living with her in whatever shit hole she called home. Or, if I had stayed in foster care and not been adopted, life could have turned out differently. I was lucky though and my parents found me and wanted me. Same with Wyatt."

"Do you remember your birth mom?" Goddamn, she could not seem to stop asking these kinds of questions.

"No and honestly, that's just fine by me. This conversation is the first time I've even thought about her in years. Who she was doesn't define who I am. I might have her genetic makeup but I have way more of my mom and dad inside me. My adopted mom and dad. Although to me, they are just mom and dad."

"God, you're so well adjusted and here I am all fucked up when my path in life was a lot easier."

He was quiet for a few seconds before finally saying, "I don't think a person's path can determine whether they are happy or unhappy. Sometimes the person who grows up in the best family with money and opportunities is the person who ends up with problems. There are no guarantees."

She thought about that and wondered if what he was saying was true. And if it was, did that mean she'd caused her own problems?

"This is a pretty heavy conversation," he said.

"Not quite what you had in mind when you called me, is it?

"Doesn't matter to me. I just like talking to you."

She felt herself smile as she sighed into the phone. "You're really good for my ego."

"I like to hear you laugh. You do it so rarely, and I have to tell you, it's the best sound I've ever heard."

"You really don't get out much do you?" She laughed and she could have sworn she heard him groan.

"You could help me with that by agreeing to go out with me."

"I thought I already had?"

"Tomorrow night?"

It was on the tip of her tongue to shout out YES, but she held back and made him wait for her answer. "That might be possible."

He chuckled. "You don't give an inch. How's seven?"

"I can make seven work."

"I'll pick you up then." There was a pause. "Thanks for talking to me."

She didn't want their conversation to end, but knew that it had to. Shockingly, she liked talking to him more than she'd ever thought she would. "Night, Flynn." Slowly she lowered her phone from her ear, hitting the end button.

Steading her breathing, she closed her eyes and began to replay their whole conversation over and over in her head. She liked him. A lot. And that scared the ever-loving shit out of her.

She wasn't used to liking guys. Wanting them? Sure. But enjoying conversations? That was totally new.

And something she had no experience with.

Chapter 8

Flynn had been smiling all day.

He couldn't help it. Talking to Joy had been energizing. After months of wondering if he'd imagined her fun and friendly that night, he finally had proof that she was that way. And that laugh...fuck it did things to him. Things like making him want to hear it for the rest of his life.

Which was fucking crazy.

He hadn't even kissed her yet – something he was planning to rectify that night – and they'd barely even touched.

The way he was feeling though, when they did finally have physical contact, he was going to go up in flames.

Standing, he dusted himself off from where he'd been installing some electrical in a bathroom. Looking around, he saw that all his employees had cleaned up and left for the day. He wasn't sure when that had happened and how he hadn't noticed. Pulling out his phone, he checked the time and noticed it was after six.

"Shit!" he swore. He had less than an hour to get the truck back to the office, go home to shower and change, before picking up Joy.

On one of the most important days of his life, he was going to be fucking late.

He bypassed cleaning up, which was something he never did and gathered all his tools quickly. In his truck, he drummed his fingers on the steering wheel as he drove as fast as he could to the office. Normally he'd empty the truck and reload it for the next day, but not tonight. He pulled inside the warehouse and jumped out of the cab. Finding the keys to his own truck in his office, he locked up the shop and jumped in.

When he was finally home, he had less than thirty minutes to shower, change and leave. He'd be cutting it close but there was no way he was allowing himself to be late. Joy deserved better. Sure, he could text and explain, but he didn't want her to think she wasn't important. Nor did he want her to know that he'd been running late because he'd been daydreaming about her.

With damp hair and sweat on his forehead, he knocked on her door with two minutes to spare. And when she opened it, his mind went blank.

She was gorgeous.

A pale yellow sundress covered her body, but showed just enough to have him salivating. Her hair was down, which it never was, and she was smiling.

The smile was what did him in.

She never smiled and that she was doing it for him...well, he was blown away.

"Hi," she said happily.

He swallowed. "You are," he shook his head. "you take my breath away."

She put her hands on her hips and eyed him speculatively. "Is this date Flynn?"

He half-grinned. "There's not much difference between date Flynn and regular Flynn. I'm pretty much the same person."

"You mean you don't compliment your date just because?"

"Never. If I say something, it's because I mean it."

"Give me a sec." She left the door open and he watched as she grabbed her purse and keys. Closing the door behind her, he stepped back so she could lock it. "Where are we headed?"

"I thought maybe we could go into Woodridge, but if you'd rather stay here, we could."

They walked side-by-side to his truck. "Woodridge works for me."

He opened the door for her, but she paused before getting inside, turning to face him. "Your hair's still wet." Her head was tilted and she pulled her bottom lip into her mouth.

"Yeah, I was running a little behind, and had to shower quickly in order to pick you up on time."

He saw her hand out of the corner of his eye as it lifted, getting closer and closer to his head. When her fingers touched his scalp under his wet hair, he practically groaned. Then her hand slid down his face as she ran her fingers through his beard, and this time, he did groan.

Her eyes never left his and he was mesmerized by their depth. "It means a lot that you weren't late. Consideration for other people is a huge turn on."

Fuck. He wasn't going to make it if she said things like that. Reaching up, he gripped her wrist with his hand. "I'm trying to be good here, Joy. I'm trying to take it slow and make sure you know I want more than one night. More than sex. But, when you touch me or say things like that, it's really fucking hard."

She visibly swallowed but her eyes stayed on his. "I don't know how to do this. Date. I've never done it, but I want to try with you. Maybe you could try to tone down the sexy?"

A laugh bubbled out. "Only if you do the same."

Her lips turned up in a smile. "Should I go back in and put on a paper sack?"

"It wouldn't help. Your sexiness comes from your smile and your laugh. The rest of you," he glanced down between them, "is just icing on the cake."

"Now look who's saying things that make it hard to be good." She winked as she dropped her hand and turned to climb into his truck. He could only stare as her ass and legs came into view.

Was it possible to have a heart attack before age thirty? Although, maybe if he did, she'd give him mouth-to-mouth.

It might be worth it.

During the drive into Woodridge, he handed her his phone and told her to pick the music.

As she flipped through his playlists, she commented, "You like country?"

"I do. I also like other things."

"I'm pretty versatile too. Country is my first love, but recently I've gotten into older R&B."

"There might be some of that on there."

The truck soon filled with the beats of an old sixties tune that he knew well. She sang under her breath and he joined in even though his voice was not meant for singing.

One song moved into another and soon they were pulling into the restaurant having driven mostly the whole way in comfortable silence.

"I'm guessing I told you that I like Thai food during that conversation we had."

"You did. Is this okay?"

She laughed and shook her head. "It's fucking perfect."

"Why does that not sound like a compliment?"

"It's just a little unnerving when I don't remember anything that I told you. I now, at least remember the things you said, but I am clueless as to what I told you."

He opened his door. "I can make that easy on you and tell you." He stepped out and when she started to open her door he stopped her. "I'll come around."

When he opened her door, she didn't get out right away but her head was turned sideways to look at him.

"Something wrong?"

And then she smiled and stepped out, taking his hand for help. "I think I might like dating you."

Confused by her comment, but happy that she was smiling and holding his hand, he led them inside. "I refuse to question anything that makes you smile."

"I just didn't know that the whole opening the door for a girl was a real thing. It threw me off for a second."

That made him pause. Sure, he'd heard her say that she'd never dated, but it never occurred to him what that meant. But, if a guy had never opened a car door for her, then she was missing out.

"Are you coming?" she asked, still holding his hand.

Nodding, he picked up his feet and started walking again. Because it was mid-week, the place wasn't busy making it easy to get a table.

"I want to start by saying that I don't think you divulged any state secrets the night we talked."

She rolled her eyes, but there was a smile on her face. "To someone who doesn't like to talk about herself, anything could be a state secret."

He wanted to ask why she didn't talk about herself, but decided at the last second, to let it go. For now.

"Remember this was before Avery and Dax were together, so I didn't know either of you. You told me about your twin sister and how she was the steady one and you were the flighty one. Which by the way, I don't think is true at all." When she looked like she was ready to interrupt, he kept going. "You talked about your job and how much you love what you do. You also mentioned that someday, you wanted to own your own salon."

She looked down at the table and began to play with her spoon. "I can't believe I told you that. You were a stranger."

"Once we started talking, it was almost as if both of us had things we wanted to talk about but didn't have anyone to actually talk to."

"But you have friends and family to talk to. And I don't remember anything you said being so...big."

"Maybe it's not big to you but it could have been to me."

She drummed her fingers on the table. "I know your favorite color and the song you love the most. I know that you love The Office and watch it non-stop if there is nothing else on. You told me about your parents and how much you love them and your brother, but even loving them that much, you felt like you had to leave." Her fingers stopped moving. "That's it, isn't it? The moving thing?"

He held her gaze and nodded. It impressed him that she could figure it out so easily. "My mom and dad understood why I needed to go, but it was still hard after everything they'd done for me. But, I just needed to get out of there. Make something of myself without them having a hand in it."

"Know that you were enough."

He blinked several times and then they just stared at each other across the table. Of course she got it, got him. That was why it had been so easy to talk to her that night in December. Her empathy had been evident and he'd needed that. He needed someone to understand how it felt.

She was looking down at the table, but when he spoke, she looked up. "I like that you get me." His voice was low and hoarse and sounded weird even to his own ears.

"This is crazy."

"What is?"

"How...connected I feel to you. How much I like you. How much I want to tear off your shirt and lick your chest."

"If I get a vote, I think you should definitely do the last one."

A smile lit up her face. "I'm on a sex sabbatical, so there will be no licking of any kind."

"I can wait."

She shook her head and threw an arm up in the air. "And that's why."

Laughing, he picked up his glass and took a sip of his beer. He knew they were moving into dangerous territory talking about sex, but it was just so easy to talk to her. About anything. Even sex.

"How long have you been on this sabbatical?" It was a crazy question to ask. He didn't give a shit if it was yesterday.

She lowered her gaze to the table as she ran her finger around the rim of her wine glass. "That's a hard question to answer."

He squinted and sat back. "Elaborate."

"I mean, the last time I kissed someone was in February, but the last time I had sex," she bit her lip looking up at him through hooded lashes, "that was December."

He couldn't look away nor could he breathe. December was when they'd met. Was it just a coincidence that she hadn't had sex since then? It had to be.

Right?

"I kept going out," she continued on, "and I'd meet guys, but for some reason, I couldn't go through with it. I didn't know why. Until Monday night." Her eyes were darting back and forth between him and the table.

"Hey," he said when he could finally form words again, "look at me." He reached across the table and took her hand in his. When her eyes lifted to his, all he saw was heat making him wonder if his looked the same to her. "Not that it matters, but it's been the same for me."

"Do you think that means we are just two horny people who want to get laid?"

Rubbing his thumb over the back of her hand, he laughed. "That's probably true, but I know that's not the only reason you are all I can think about."

Before she could say anything, their waiter walked up to take their orders. He dropped her hand, picking up his menu. He'd completely forgotten what he'd planned to order.

"Tell me about your dad?" he asked when the waiter walked away. They needed a change of subject and this was his chance.

"What about him? He died when I was five, so I hardly remember him."

"That's not what you told me before. You told me how much you loved him and how it broke you when he died."

Her eyes widened for a second before she slowly shook her head and smiled. "I really am going to need a list of everything I told you." She took a sip of her wine. "Unlike Avery, my dad and I got along great.

I loved to sit in his office and just watch him pour over papers and files. And he liked having me there. I think it was because I didn't bother him. But, if Avery was in there, she would ask a ton of questions that would annoy him."

"I know parents aren't supposed to have favorite kids, but I think they do, and I also think it's okay. I never annoyed my mom quite as much as Wyatt did, but with my dad, Wyatt could do no wrong. Sometimes certain personalities just work better together." Like theirs. He looked over the table at her beautiful smile. It made his heart beat faster making him wonder if it would always be that way.

"You're so wise. You could give Julia a run for her money."

"I appreciate the vote of confidence but I like my job and what I do. Plus, I don't think I am any wiser than most people. I just know the people in my life."

Once their food arrived, they continued to talk comfortably all through their meal. When they walked out of the restaurant, he was surprised when she reached for his hand. It felt so good to touch her and that she'd been the one to initiate contact, made his heart swell in his chest. He opened the passenger side door and reluctantly let go of her hand as she climbed inside. Closing the door, he took several deep breaths to control all his pent up desire for her. He didn't want to do anything that would pressure her or that would make her change her mind about him.

He had just pulled away from the parking lot when he felt her hand reach across and touch his on the gear shift. He glanced across the seat to her and smiled as he entwined his fingers with hers resting them on the center console. It felt like only minutes had passed when he pulled up in front of her apartment complex.

He again opened the door for her and then they walked up the sidewalk to her door.

"As second dates go, this one was pretty good." She turned as they reached her door.

"I'm glad I lived up to your standards."

"Thanks again." She turned to insert her key in the lock.

When he heard the lock click and then the door opened, he knew that if he was going to kiss her, it had to be now.

"Joy," he said in a whisper, his fingertips touching her.

Slowly, she turned back to face him, her eyes wide, her bottom lip caught between her teeth. He moved in closer, his hand coming up to caress her neck and cheek.

"I want to kiss you so fucking bad." He smoothed her bottom lip with his thumb. "But I don't want to rush you."

She swallowed, but never took her eyes off his. He could feel her warm breath against his thumb and that alone had him aroused.

He was fucking gone for this woman.

She moved even closer to him. That had to be a good sign, right? Lifting her own hand to his bearded face, she said, "You're not rushing me."

Those words were all he needed to hear before he closed the distance between them, touching his lips to hers. At the first touch it was like an electrical current coursing through his whole body. She tasted of wine and Thai spices and every bit of sweetness he dreamed she'd taste like. When his tongue swept into her mouth, she moaned, leaning in closer, her hand moving up to grip his hair. His own arms circled around her lower back, his fingers resting just above her ass.

He was lost in the feel of her. Finally, she was in his arms, kissing him back like he'd dreamed about so many times the last six months.

Slowing the kiss, he pulled back just enough to look in her eyes. They were both breathing heavily and there was no way she couldn't feel the evidence of his arousal against her stomach. "Thank you for going out with me." It was corny, but because she'd been hesitant to go out with him, he felt it needed to be said.

She licked her lips and he held in a groan. "Thank you for not wanting to rush me," she ran her fingers through his hair, "and for that kiss." She dropped her hands from his hair and stepped out of his embrace. "Goodnight, Flynn."

He continued to watch her until she was inside her apartment and he heard the door lock. Stepping forward, he braced both his hands against the frame and dropped his head forward, being careful not to let it hit the door. He didn't want her to come back out there. Well, he did, but if she did, he might not be able to stop himself from kissing her again. Only for longer this time. And naked.

Yeah, he didn't need her to come out there.

Minutes passed before he regained enough control to walk away. He'd just had the best date and best kiss of his life and now he had to go home alone.

Alone, where he would spend the whole night thinking of things he had no business thinking about.

Things like Joy as his wife where they were in love and starting a family.

Things he wanted so badly that nothing else seemed to matter.

Chapter 9

Two days of sweet, cute, and fun text messages led to two nights of tossing and turning.

She and Flynn had both been too busy to set a second—or third as he kept saying—date, so instead, they'd texted each other. He was busy helping Dax finish up a project so there'd be less work while Dax was gone on his honeymoon and she'd doubled up her clients since she was taking both Friday and Saturday off to help Avery with wedding prep.

That's where she was headed. To Avery's house, where a group of them were gathering before heading off to Woodridge for a day of pampering. It had been a while since she'd had her own mani and pedi. She painted her toes, but rarely did she actually get a full pedicure. Her nails though, she never did them. They just got ruined when she did other people's nails.

Avery and Dax weren't doing any kind of rehearsal dinner so she wouldn't see Flynn until tomorrow.

And she couldn't wait. With him in mind, she'd purchased the sexiest dress she could find. It was yellow, long, strapless, and there was a slit that went all the way up to her mid-thigh.

She was hoping that at some point he'd utilize that slit.

As she pulled into Avery's drive, she wondered again if she should tell her sister about Flynn. She wanted to, but she also wanted to keep him to herself. But, she hated lying. Plus, she hadn't said anything to Flynn about not telling Avery, so it was very possible he'd already told Dax. Deciding she should find out before she made a decision, she sent him a quick text before getting out of the car.

Joy:

Have you told Dax about us?

Flynn:

About us talking? I think he knows we do that.

Joy:

Don't be an ass. You know what I'm talking about.
Flynn:
*No, I haven't said anything. I wanted to make sure you were okay with
me saying something.*
Joy:
I think I might tell Avery today. I don't like lying to her.
Flynn:
So I can tell my friends?
Joy:
Have at it.
Flynn:
I'm looking forward to seeing you tomorrow.

She didn't answer back, instead, she shoved her phone in her purse as she was getting out of the car. She passed by Julia's car, which wasn't surprising, since she was always early for everything. Addison, Leah, Carly, and Melanie would also be joining them.

She walked right in without knocking. Wasn't that a perk of having a sister? "Let the fun begin!" she shouted as she entered.

"The fun started ten minutes ago," Julia said, lifting what looked like a mimosa in the air in salute.

"You know, being early is not really what people consider fun."

Julia flipped her off as she took a sip of her drink, making Joy laugh. "Where's the bride to be?"

"Right here," Avery said, walking into the room. "Just a last minute wardrobe change thanks to Thunder jumping on me and his toenail tearing a hole in my shirt."

"Where is the little guy?" She looked around but didn't see Thunder anywhere.

"Dax took him to his mom's place for the weekend. It would just be too hard to have him here with all the people around. Plus, he's staying with her while we are gone."

Joy raised her eyebrows at Avery's words. "I take it Dax told you about your surprise honeymoon?"

"Oh yeah, that man cannot keep a secret."

There was a knock at the door just before it opened and Leah, Addison, Carly, and Melanie all entered. "Happy almost wedding day!" Addison bellowed.

"How is it," Leah said, "that I was the first to have a boyfriend, and, yet I am the last one to get married.

"You're the idiot who wanted to wait so long," Carly said. "I told you it was a stupid idea."

Carly and Tony had the first wedding with a surprise appearance by Addison and Ryan. Then, of course, Julia and Wes had an impromptu wedding a week after getting engaged, and now Avery and Dax were a month later. Mel and Logan had been planning their September wedding for months and then Leah and Brandon were last with a December wedding date.

Soon she would be the only single one.

And wasn't that depressing?

"What's on the agenda today?" Melanie asked.

Avery pointed to Addison. "I put Addison in charge, mainly because she begged me, so don't any of the rest of you think I like you less. I mean I do," she gave an evil smile and a wink, "but I don't want you to know that."

"I, for one, am fine with Addison being in charge," Joy spoke up. "Being the sister of the bride is hard enough without having to be in charge too."

"If you all would please shut up," Addison rubbed her growing belly as she spoke, "I'll tell you the agenda."

"Shoot," Carly said, her own baby bump too small to see yet.

What the fuck was in the water in this town?

"Facials are first followed by massages and then mani's and pedi's. Afterward, we have a late lunch at The Sun Deck. I reserved the upstairs so we can be as loud and obnoxious as we want. After, we will head out on the boat for a fun afternoon ride complete with drinks and snacks. Then dinner back here."

"There's a small change in the dinner." Avery said. "Dax and I wanted to do that together, so all the guys will be joining us. And Wes being the amazing guy that he is, has offered to pre-make the food and bring it."

Joy kept her face neutral at the news that she'd get to see Flynn that night. Inside she was doing the cha-cha. Sure, it was a bad cha-cha, but it was still the cha-cha.

"My husband is pretty awesome," Julia said. "Oh and you guys should see the cakes that Dani made both for tonight and for tomorrow. That girl has a way with desserts."

"Feel free to keep talking," Addison said, "but, maybe let's do it in the car."

Joy was surprised to find out that Carly had borrowed her aunt's SUV so they could all ride together. She squeezed in the back, along with Avery, since they had the shortest legs. It was cramped, but they were both short so they easily fit.

This might be as good a time as any to tell Avery about Flynn. She turned inward and kept her voice low. "I went on a date with Flynn."

Avery who had been rummaging through her purse stopped and looked up at her. "You what?"

"I went on a date with Flynn. I mean it's two dates if you ask him, but really it's just the one, because the first one doesn't really count since we were both there separately. But, he insists that because we sat next to each other, had a conversation, and then he paid, that it was a date. Sometimes the man is infuriating."

She put her hand up, in a *stop talking* gesture. "Flynn Murray? The one who works for Dax?"

She nodded, afraid to speak for fear she'd say something stupid.

Avery made a face that she had been making since she was five. Joy knew it well. It was her thinking face. After a few seconds, the face was gone, replaced by a smile. "Okay."

"Okay? That's it?" She had been for sure that Avery would have a comment or concern.

"Joy, it's your life. Who you date or don't date is really none of my business unless he treats you badly. And if I had to guess, Flynn treats you very well."

She blinked at the sexual innuendo. "We've only been on the one real date so I can't really say."

"Oh come on. This is Flynn. He's all hot and sexy and smoldering. He's definitely going to give you his all."

Leah, who was in the middle row along with Julia and Mel, turned around. "Are you talking about lumberjack Flynn? God that man is hot." She fanned her face.

"It seems my sister here has been keeping secrets. She and Flynn are dating."

Julia also turned her head. "You did it? Went on a date with Flynn?"

"You knew?" Avery asked Julia.

Julia looked from Joy to Avery and then back to Joy. "Sorry," she whispered.

"It's fine. Yes, she knew," she said to Avery. "She was there the night Flynn asked me out."

"We all knew you liked him," Carly shouted from the driver's seat. "That part isn't really news, is it?"

"It is to me," Avery said. "Not that I care. I like Flynn." She looked over to Joy. "But, I would have liked to know that my sister had a crush."

"It wasn't a crush so much as an avoidance of the hot guy who couldn't take his eyes off her," Julia said. "Now Flynn, he totally had a crush."

"Why can't a bearded hottie have a crush on me?" Addison said.

"Maybe because you're married and currently pregnant," Melanie said. "Plus, it's not as if Ryan isn't hot in his own right."

"I'm with Addison," Leah said. "Flynn is on a different level of the hotness scale. His eyes, that beard and, oh my God, that body," she actually licked her lips, "Joy, you are one lucky woman."

"Do your husbands and fiancè know that you guys sit around and drool over Flynn? I'd be happy to inform them." She was laughing because this conversation was so absurd.

"Don't even think about it!" Avery shouted.

"Girl code assures us that you will keep your mouth shut," Carly yelled from the front.

She rolled her eyes. "I'm not sure about dating a guy that all my friends find fuckable."

"You're kidding right?" Leah said. "Girl, that is the dream."

"How is that the dream?"

"Hello," Addison said. "When all your friends want the guy, that means everyone else does too, but guess what, he belongs to you. Even better, he loves you and would do anything for you."

"Um, Flynn doesn't love me. We've been on one date."

"Metaphorically," Julia said. "It is pretty empowering knowing that people are looking at your guy when all he can look at is you."

"So what's the deal with you guys then?" Melanie asked. "Are you going on another date? Oh, have you kissed, or wait...have you slept together?"

"The date was Tuesday, but we've both been really busy since then. We said we'd meet at the wedding tomorrow." She paused. "Yes, we kissed, but that's it."

"How was it?" Avery asked, eyes wide in question.

She scratched the back of her neck. "It's been two-and-a-half days and it's still all I can think about."

"Fucking Flynn," Carly said. "That's how it was with Anthony. I was ruined the moment he kissed me."

"Same," several of them said at the same time.

"When Dax kissed me," Avery said, "I came alive in a way I didn't know I was missing. He made me stronger and happier than I'd ever thought possible, with just that one damn kiss."

She was all dreamy-eyed, making Joy remember what this day was about. "Are you nervous at all for tomorrow?"

"Nope," she said definitively. "Dax loves me and I love him. I know without a doubt that will never change."

Joy turned to stare out the window. What would that feel like? To know that someone loves you that much and to love them back the same? She wanted that. She wanted to be the one for someone.

Could that be Flynn?

She was starting to think that maybe it was.

She'd never felt the way she had with him.

Happy. Ridiculously so.

Plus, she'd never wanted anyone the way she wanted him. That could just be because it had been so long since she'd had sex, but she didn't think so. It was Flynn. He was the one she wanted.

By the time they'd pulled up to the spa, she had talked herself in and out of a relationship with Flynn a half dozen times. She'd finally settled on going for it. What did she have to lose?

Facials were first on the list and she was both nervous and excited. She'd never had a facial, hell, she'd never done a lot of things. Money had been tight after her mom had died, so extras were out of the question. Now, though, she was an adult who made her own money. If she wanted to indulge here and there, she could. And her sister's wedding was the perfect time for indulgence.

After her facial, she was led to a room for her massage. Their group had to be separated into two smaller groups to accommodate all of them, so she ended up in a room with Carly and Julia.

"I'm so excited about this," Julia said. "It's been months since I've had a massage."

"Me too," Carly said. "And with pregnancy I wasn't sure if I could, but my doctor said as long as the massage therapist knows how to do a prenatal massage, I am good."

"I've never had a massage before," Joy said, as she positioned herself on the table.

Julia lifted up onto her elbows. "You're in for a treat. This is the most relaxed you'll ever be."

The door opened and the three female massage therapists walked in. Within minutes Joy was transported into a state of total bliss. She wasn't sure she'd ever felt that relaxed. As she floated into a half-sleep, Flynn took over her thoughts. But it wasn't complicated. More joyful. His smile and the way it felt when he touched her. The laugh he let out when he made fun of her and the looks he gave her that made her practically melt into a puddle.

In her relaxed state, all she could think of was Flynn and how happy she felt when he was around.

She was sad when her hour was up, afraid that all the happiness she felt toward him would disappear. But it didn't. Not through her pedicure or her manicure and not through lunch where they laughed, ate and drank. Then, on the way to Addison's where they'd hop on the pontoon boat, her phone vibrated in her purse.

Flynn:

I just found out that I get to see you tonight.

Joy:

I heard that same rumor.

Flynn:

Don't freak but you're all I can think about today.

Joy:

Just today?

Flynn:

Well no, but I thought you'd run for the hills if I said you were all I ever think about.

Joy:

Before my massage I might have but now I'm all Zen and shit.

Flynn:

I don't think you can say Zen and shit in the same sentence.

Joy:

Since you might reap the rewards of how Zen I am, you might not want to make fun of me.

Flynn:

Are you trying to make me hard in front of a group of guys? Do you know how that's going to look?

Joy:

See you later, Flynn.

Smiling, she filed out of the SUV with everyone else and walked down to the dock at Addison and Ryan's.

"What are you so happy about?" Leah said, walking up beside her.

She shrugged but continued to smile. She couldn't stop herself. "I think that massage flipped a switch inside me or something. All I can think about now is fun and happy things. It's like all the bad stuff has disappeared."

She nodded her head slowly. "They can do that to you. It's like your body has been waiting for a way to release all the stress."

"I wish someone had told me about this years ago. I could have saved myself a lot of grief."

Laughing, Leah patted her on the back. "I don't think it works like that for everyone. Maybe you were just more stressed than the rest of us."

That was probably true. She'd held in all her emotions and feelings for years. But no more. All she wanted now was to be happy. Oh, and maybe Flynn.

Yeah, she definitely wanted him. And, she had a hunch that he would make her very happy.

By the time the boat ride was over and they were docking, Joy could see a group of men already gathered on the back deck of Addison and Ryan's house. Ryan, along with Brandon, jogged down to help them carry the food and cooler back up to the house. Joy took her time walking, scanning the crowd for Flynn. She didn't see him anywhere at first, but then, he stepped through the sliding glass door and out onto the deck, his eyes meeting hers instantly.

Her steps faltered, making her almost trip. Smooth was not her middle name. She caught his gaze again and his grin was even wider, like maybe he was laughing at her. But she didn't care.

He began walking across the deck and then down the steps, heading straight for her. When they were mere feet apart, they both stopped.

"You look...different. Happier."

The smile that hadn't left since they'd departed the spa was still plastered on her face. "I feel happy. Maybe for the first time in a long time."

"You should smile all the time."

"I'm going to work on it." She indicated to his hands where he was holding two beers. "Is one of those for me?"

"Oh yeah," he held one out to her, "I thought you might want one."

"Good looking, smart, sexy, funny, and a mind reader. You might be too good to be true." Her fingers brushed his as she took the can from his hand. She held the connection a little longer than was needed, but it didn't seem like he cared.

Clearing his throat, he asked, "Should we join the rest of the group?"

"Probably." Still neither moved from where they were. Finally, she stepped forward, took his free hand in hers and started walking.

He looked down between them at their joined hands. "Did you tell Avery?"

"Mmhmm."

"That's all I get?"

"What else is there to say? She likes you, as does everyone else. It seems I'm the only one who took forever to realize what a good guy you were."

He was silent for a few seconds as they continued to walk.

"I like that you took your time. It means you've thought it through and I'm not an impulse."

She laughed. "If you only knew how impulsive I want to be with you." She let go of his hand and walked ahead of him up the steps. When she looked back, he was still standing at the bottom, his mouth hanging open. Shaking her head, she kept going, leaving him where he stood. She'd shocked him with her words, which had been her intention.

Now, if only she was brave enough to act on those words.

Chapter 10

Downing his beer in one long drink, Flynn closed his eyes and wondered what the hell kind of magic was performed at a spa. Joy was like a different person. And, while he'd liked the person she was just fine, he liked seeing her happy even more.

Ascending the porch steps, he dropped his empty beer can in the garbage can before reaching into the cooler and picking up another one. Joy had gone inside the house and he wanted nothing more than to follow her, but he thought better of it and walked over to where Wes and Dax were standing with Avery and Julia.

"You've been keeping secrets," Dax said, one eyebrow raised in questioning.

"I knew," Wes said, "so it wasn't really a secret."

Flynn finally understood what they were talking about. Joy. "It wasn't as if I hid my attraction to her all that well."

"You must have," Avery said, "because I had no clue."

"That's because you weren't paying attention," Julia said. "I noticed it almost immediately. That, and the fact that Joy worked way too hard to stay away from you."

"It's your job to notice things like that," Dax said. "Why didn't you tell me?" he asked Flynn.

He shrugged. "I was waiting until there was something to tell."

"Is there? Something to tell?"

He shifted his weight from one foot to the other. "I guess you could say we are dating."

"Since when?"

"Monday night," Julia spoke up before he could. "And it might be the best first date in the history of first dates."

He felt a blush climb up his face. "She still likes to say it wasn't a date."

Wes slapped him on the back. "You know I love her like she's my little sister, but I have to tell you, she's not an easy woman. She has opinions on everything."

"That's one of the things I like about her." He glanced behind him to see if he could see her. "Could we maybe stop talking about this now?" She would hate it if she knew that they were standing around talking about her.

He listened to them talk for a few more minutes before stepping away. Wes had pre-cooked everything earlier in the day and all the food was set up inside. Deciding that eating was a good excuse to go inside to see if he could find Joy, he stepped into the house. He didn't see her anywhere, nor did he see anyone else.

Setting his beer down on the counter, he walked down the hallway to see if he could find her. She wasn't in any of the rooms upstairs or the bathrooms. That left only the basement. The door was open and the light was on, but he didn't hear anything. Quietly, he walked down the stairs. As he turned the corner, he saw her. She was leaning against the wall with her back to him so she didn't see him yet. As he stepped off the last stair, she must have heard something because she turned.

She didn't say anything as he continued to walk toward her. "Are you okay?"

"I just needed to get away for a bit."

He looked back toward the stairs. "It can be a lot being with people all day."

She sighed and reached for him, her hand grabbing his. "You always seem to get me."

He lifted his free hand, tracing her jaw with his fingertips. "I've been studying you from afar for a long time." Because she was so short and he was so tall, their faces were practically aligned as he stared down at her.

"Stalker," she said as her hand came up to caress his beard. "Do you have any clue just how fucking sexy this beard is on you?"

"I don't actually think of myself as sexy."

"You should since pretty much every woman in this town thinks you're hot." Her eyes widened and she slapped the hand that had been in his beard over her mouth.

"What?"

"Nothing," she said, but it was muffled by her hand.

Using his own hand, he pulled hers away from her mouth. "You can't just say something like that and then leave me hanging."

She started laughing and shaking her head. "When I told Avery about you, the others started chiming in, and all of them think you are hot. That's it. Don't get a big head."

He wasn't sure what to think about that. He'd never seen himself as hot. Decent looking yes, but that was it. "What about you? Do you think I'm hot?" He pulled her even closer to him.

"I'm not answering that." She smiled up at him.

"What if I went first and told you that I think you are so fucking hot and sexy?"

Her breathing sped up and she visibly swallowed. His dirty mind went right to thinking about her swallowing something else. "If you were to say that I might be able to concede and tell you that I dream of you. In particular, I dream of what your beard would feel like between my legs."

He swore he stopped breathing for a second. He'd never done the dirty talk thing with a woman. It had never felt right and he'd never been comfortable enough with them. This though, with Joy, felt one hundred percent right, and he badly wanted to tell her every little thing he was thinking of doing to her.

He leaned in, rubbing his hair covered cheek against her bare one. "I would imagine it would feel like this, only more sensitive."

Her breath hitched, making him hard as stone. Turning his face, his lips brushed over hers lightly. "Look at me," he asked, his voice raw with emotion. She opened her eyes, staring into his. "I want the same things you want. I want to hear you cry out my name when my head is between your legs and your taste is on my lips. I want to kiss you after going down on you with your smell covering my beard. I want..." his next words were cut off by her lips crashing against his mouth. She'd wrapped her arm around his neck and pulled him to her. But he wasn't complaining. Kissing her was all he'd thought about since the first time he'd done it. Well, that, and stripping her naked to make love to her on his bed.

Having her in his bed was one thing he wanted more than anything. There had never been a woman in his bed, or his new house, for that matter. He wanted her to be the first, and possibly, the last.

Needing more, he ran both his hands up her rib cage, stopping only when his thumbs grazed the underside of her breasts. She shivered against him, pulling him even closer. Needing more friction, he moved them both so her back was up against the wall. Immediately, she clung to him tighter, wrapping her legs around his waist. Groaning into her mouth, he moved his hands to her ass to help hold her in place.

Neither let up on the kiss. They both seemed to need more, and they were both taking what they wanted. He pressed her tighter into the wall, his hard cock connecting directly with her core. When he felt her swivel her hips, he almost came, and somehow, that snapped him back to reality.

"Joy," he murmured, moving his lips along her jaw, "we have to stop."

"I don't want to," she whispered, her voice heavy. "You make me feel so good."

"Is this really what you want? Us fucking up against the wall in the basement while a party is going on above us?"

"Well, when you put it like that," she paused, and a huge smile appeared, "yes, that's really what I want."

He couldn't stop his laughter from bubbling out. Dropping his forehead to hers, he smoothed her hair back. "Stop tempting me. We will finish this."

"When?" She slid her legs down him until they touched the floor.

"Pack a bag and come home with me tomorrow night after the wedding?"

"Come to your place? I don't even know where you live."

"You can find out tomorrow." He bent and pressed his lips to hers. "Please?"

She sighed and rubbed her hands up and down his chest. "If I say yes now, can I reserve the right to change my mind, if say, I go crazy between now and then?"

He knew it was meant to be funny, but he also knew she needed time and that was her way of asking for it. "Always. You have all the power here."

"That could be interesting."

Somehow he gathered the strength to step away from her. "Should we go back up and join the rest of our friends?"

"Um, I don't think you can go up there like that." She looked down between them. Her eyes going right to his dick.

"If you stop staring at and talking about him, he'll go away." Probably. It was a toss-up when she was around.

"If you say so." She walked past him, her hand brushing his as she did so. Laughing, he turned and followed her up the stairs. Which did nothing to fix his rather large problem. Adjusting himself in his shorts, he took the last step into the kitchen.

Logan and Melanie were at the counter filling plates with food and spotted them coming through the door.

"I was wondering where you'd gone off to," Mel said.

"I was just taking a people break and Flynn came to find me."

"Do I look stupid?" She looked up to Logan. "Why lie, just say you were in the basement making out."

Flynn stepped around Joy. "We were in the basement making out."

Logan held up his fist and Flynn had no choice but to fist bump him.

"Guys are pigs," Mel said. "Joy, let's get out of here before they start grunting and pounding their chests."

Logan slapped her on the ass. "Love you, honey."

Melanie rolled her eyes, took Joy's hand and walked away. Joy gave him a smile and raised her eyebrows as she walked by him.

"So you and Joy, huh?" Logan took a bite of pasta as he leaned back against the counter, his ankles crossed.

"Are you going to give me the third degree?" It came out a little more angry than he'd meant it too.

"Not me." He continued to eat. "I'm just wondering if you know what you are getting into?"

"I don't think I understand?"

"Look around you, man. When people date in this town, they end up married or about to be married."

Flynn understood what he was getting at. Every single person at this party had fallen in love in less time than it took to build a house. Some instantly. That was the group he was going to end up in. Joy had him from the moment she sat down at his table and laughed six months ago.

And, for the first time, he was starting to think he might actually have a chance.

"I think I'll be fine."

"It's like that, is it?" Logan smirked as he took another bite of food.

Flynn grinned. "It's definitely like that." Picking up a plate, he began filling it with food. "How's the gallery?" Logan was a famous photographer who had recently moved back to town and opened an art gallery. The gallery held art from artists all over the world and was starting to gain recognition as a place for new and upcoming artists.

"Busy. I never thought I'd run short of room with a place that big, but it seems everyone wants me to showcase their pieces."

"That's good though, right?" Flynn had no clue how the art world worked or what was good or bad.

"Oh yeah, it's great, I just wish now that I had more space."

"I'm assuming you aren't willing to move?"

"No, that is not what I want to do."

"What about the land behind the building? You could add on to what's now the parking lot and then you could clear out some of the trees and greenery for another lot."

Logan stood up straighter. "I hadn't thought of that. I'm not sure who owns that land, but I know it's several acres."

"You should look into it."

"You are a genius, Flynn." He pushed away from the counter. "If I decide to add on, consider the job yours." Logan headed out of the kitchen and back out onto the deck.

Flynn followed him out once his plate was filled with food, his eyes immediately searching for Joy. He found her sitting on a chair talking to Addison and Avery. While he wanted badly to go to her, he also wanted her to enjoy her time. So he sat back and enjoyed the evening with his friends.

Tomorrow they would finish what they'd started in the basement.

The wedding wasn't until four, but Flynn had told Dax that he'd arrive a few hours early to help out. It wasn't going to be a big crowd, no more than twenty people, but there was still a little setup.

When he arrived, he walked around back and found Dax, sitting on the steps of the deck in shorts and a t-shirt.

"I hope that's not what you're wearing to get married?"

Raising his eyebrows, he flipped Flynn off. "I could say the same to you."

Flynn looked down at his own shorts and t-shirt. "My clothes are in the truck," he said as he sat down next to him. "Where's Wes, I thought he'd be here by now?"

"He's on the way. He was stopping to pick up the cake from his baker, Dani."

Flynn looked over at his best friend. Dax was a high strung guy, or he had been until he'd met Avery but today, he looked more like the Dax he'd known before Avery had come along. "You look nervous?"

"I am nervous." His voice was shaky. "But not about marrying Avery. It's more that I'm afraid I'll be a horrible husband, or worse, a bad father." He looked up at Flynn. "How do I know I can be what she needs?"

"Dax are you kidding? You're going to be great at both of those things. I know, because you pretty much took me in when I moved to Cedarville and made sure I stayed on the right path. You were my teacher, my mentor, and my best friend, and you did it all without ever wondering what you'd get in return. Those are the qualities of a good man. A man that Avery will be lucky to call her husband and any kid would love to call a father."

"Seems like maybe you got some of those qualities too."

"I'd like to think so, but I'll have to wait and see."

"This thing with Joy, is it serious?"

"To me it is, but she's a few steps behind."

Dax looked over to him before looking back down at the ground. "My money's on you. When you want something, you usually get it."

It didn't feel that way to him, but he really hoped his friend was right. This time the reward was too big to lose. "Let's get this place set up so your new bride doesn't kill you."

They worked side-by-side setting up tables and chairs. Wes walked in, bringing the cake, and minutes later the caterer pulled up. After getting it all set up, Dax went to shower, while he and Wes freshened up and began dressing.

Flynn rarely had reason to dress up with his job, but he did own a few nicer pieces. He'd opted for no suit since this was a casual wedding. He went with light gray pants and a white button-down, with the sleeves rolled, and no tie. It was casual, but it worked for Dax and Avery's backyard wedding.

Wes was very similarly dressed when he came out into the living room.

"Looks like we had the same idea."

He looked down at himself. "Julia asked Avery three times to make sure it was okay that I wasn't wearing a tie." He shook his head laughing. "I kept telling her that no one would care."

"I could get used to this type of wedding though. Casual is in my wheelhouse."

"Is Julia with Avery getting ready?" He knew that Joy was with her, but he hadn't thought to ask about anyone else.

"She was dressed and ready to go when I dropped her off, but her job is to make sure they are on time."

"Probably a good idea."

They both turned when Dax walked into the room. "How do I look?"

Flynn examined his friend. He was a little more formal in his black pants, multi-colored striped shirt, and pink tie. Avery loved pink.

"Looking good, man," Wes said.

"I like the shirt."

"Avery said I could wear whatever I wanted, and when I saw this shirt and tie, I figured she'd love it."

"She will," Flynn said.

They were still chatting when Logan and Melanie walked in. Logan was the official photographer, even though he was also an invited guest.

Before he even spoke, he had his camera up to his face and was snapping pictures.

"Is he always like this?" Flynn asked Mel.

"Yes, and it's annoying. I swear for years I didn't even know what his face looked like without a camera attached to it."

"So you were in love with my body," Logan said, lowering the camera, "I see how it is now."

Melanie rolled her eyes. "This is my life."

"And you love it," Wes said.

A huge smile appeared on her face. "Yeah, I do."

Flynn felt his phone buzz in his pocket. When he pulled it out, he saw it was Joy.

Joy:

Bride's here. Clear the room except for Dax and Logan for pictures.

Flynn:

On it.

"Avery's here," he announced.

"That's our cue," Melanie said, kissing Logan's cheek. "See you in a few."

She, followed by Flynn and Wes, walked out on the back deck. Just as he stepped out, Joy walked around the corner.

HIs heart stopped.

She was a fucking goddess.

Her hair was down and curled, blowing in the summer breeze. Her dress was a pale yellow that hugged her body like a second skin. There were no straps, leaving her neck and shoulders bare, but because the dress was long, her legs were covered.

And, that's when he noticed the slit on the side. It went all the way up her leg, almost to her hip.

He practically swallowed his tongue.

She was moving toward him, a smile on her freshly painted lips.

"When I bought this dress, that is exactly the look I was hoping to see on your face." She was only a few feet from him now, and his hands itched to touch.

"Were you trying to kill me, because I'm pretty sure it worked?" He couldn't stop his eyes from roaming over her, again and again.

"I was hoping," she stepped closer, a hand reaching out to touch his chest, "that you'd take one look at me and not be able to think about anything but me all day." He'd noticed that she wasn't wearing heels and that made her head come only to below his chin.

He flicked his eyes up to her face. "I think that was a given with or without the dress."

"Admit it though, the dress helps." She did a turn, giving him a glimpse of her backside.

"I'm not going to complain, that's for sure." When she was facing him again, he reached for her hand and pulled her into him, breathing in her scent. "You smell almost as good as you look."

She leaned back, looking up at him. "I should probably tell you that what you're wearing works for me." She smoothed a hand down his crisp white shirt. "Casual, yet sexy." She bit her lip then asked. "Would it be okay if I took a picture of us?"

"Only if you send it to me." That she wanted a picture of the two of them together gave him hope that he wasn't the only one in deep.

She pulled out her phone and then curled into his side with her arm out. "You're too tall."

"Here, let me take it."

"Do you know how to take a selfie?" She was mocking him and he knew it, so he just shook his head.

"I don't think it's brain surgery."

"You'd be surprised." She leaned into him again and he snapped several photos.

When she reached for the phone, he held onto her with his other arm, so she couldn't scoot away. He liked her next to him where he could touch and smell her.

"These are good." She turned the phone toward him so he could look.

"You look great."

"So do you." She examined the picture again.

"If you say so." He didn't really care what he looked like and he was pretty sure she'd always look great in photos. "Just make sure you send me one." He looked down at her and closed the distance. "Are we still on for tonight?"

Her eyes searched his and somehow they ended up even closer together. "My mind is telling me I should slow this down but my heart and my body want to jump in with both feet."

He dropped his forehead to hers, caressing her cheek with his hand. "We can go slow, as slow as you need. I'm not going anywhere, Joy. I know you aren't where I am, but I can wait, I will wait."

Her eyes widened. "Where are you?"

"Halfway in love with you." He'd opted for honesty, even though that wasn't the whole truth. He was closer to all the way in love with her, but she wasn't ready to hear that.

Closing her eyes, she took a steadying breath. When she opened them back up, she was smiling. "You overwhelm me, Flynn, but in a good way. In a way that makes me think that maybe, just maybe, I should follow my heart and not my brain." She leaned even closer until her lips lightly touched his. The kiss was sweet and gentle but packed a hell of a punch. "Tonight, we can work on that."

Stepping away from him, she straightened her dress before giving him one last look and walking away.

He watched her go and wondered – not for the first time – how crazy fate was.

Chapter 11

Flynn scrambled her brain.

And, for some reason, she freaking loved it.

Ever since last night when she'd practically forced herself on him in Addison's basement, she couldn't stop thinking about him. About how his hands felt touching her or how his beard was scratchy against her skin. Oh, who was she kidding? She hadn't been able to stop thinking about him since that night, so long ago in December, even if she hadn't remembered it.

Now though, it was different. Now she knew that he wanted her, that he liked her, and more than that, she liked him. And boy, did she like him. Really though, who wouldn't? The man was nice. Not only that, but he seemed to get her. Those were qualities she wasn't used to. Qualities she couldn't seem to resist.

Glancing back up to the deck where he continued to stand, she took him in. He was casually dressed, but still managed to look like a million bucks. The white shirt against his tan skin had her salivating, and while he still had the beard, she could easily see that it had been trimmed.

If possible, she liked it even more.

Her lips were still tingling from where she'd lightly kissed him. Swiping her tongue along her bottom one, she swore she tasted him.

She desperately wanted another taste.

Because of that, she headed around the front of the house, away from Flynn—and temptation—and ran into Julia.

"Whoa, what's the hurry?"

"No hurry," she glanced behind her to make sure Flynn hadn't followed her, "just wanted to check on things."

"Or, maybe you're hiding from Flynn?"

"Why would I be hiding from Flynn?" Sure she was, but why would Julia think that?

"Oh I don't know, maybe because you are still sorting through all your issues and he scares you because you know he's serious."

"You know, you're really smug and it's pretty damn annoying."

"I'm only smug when I'm right, which, in this case, I am."

"Okay, so yes, he scares me. On the surface he seems to be everything I ever dreamed of, but can I trust that? Will he change down the road and become someone else?"

"Like your dad did with your mom?"

Joy closed her eyes, the memory of the day after her dad died flooding her head. She'd been crying non-stop along with Avery and their mom. Then her mom took a phone call, and all of a sudden, she went from crying to screaming. Joy had never seen her mom so angry. She was in her dad's office throwing papers everywhere and using every bad word that Joy had heard at the young age of five, plus a few she'd never heard. She was too young to understand at the time, but as the years went on, she finally got what her dad had done. He'd left them without anything. No money, no house, nothing. Even worse, her mom had been responsible for a lot of his debt.

They'd had to move to an apartment and her mom had to work 7 days a week just to keep up with the bills. All because her dad had lied.

She had already been sad and upset when her dad had died, but when she found out that he wasn't the person she'd thought he was, she'd shut down. At the young age of eight, she'd sworn to herself that no man would ever have the power to let her down. And until Flynn, until right that minute, she'd kept that promise.

Only now, she wasn't sure the promise was one she should keep. She was starting to realize that not all men were bad and that not all of them wanted control.

"I think I am starting to understand that not everyone was like my dad. It's not an easy thing to let go of, something you've been holding onto for almost twenty years.."

Julia stepped closer, putting a hand on Joy's arm. "I think if you look around at your friends, you'll see that relationships are a two-way street. What your dad did to you and your family is not the norm. Love and respect are more normal than you might think."

"This is a heavy conversation for a day that is supposed to be happy."

"I think Avery would also want you happy on this day, so the conversation is warranted. Don't let your past dictate your future. Flynn likes you. A lot. And, from what I can see, you like him."

"I'm going home with him tonight."

Julia blinked, a big smile forming on her face. "You know, that was news you could have told me five minutes ago."

"I don't know if I'm ready for sex. Okay that's a lie, I want sex more than I want cake, and I fucking love cake. But, what I do know is that being with him, in any way, makes me feel good. It's been so long since I've felt good. Maybe since my dad died."

"Well then, consider this my prescription to you for fun. Tonight, whatever you decide to do or not do with Flynn, just make sure you're having fun."

Smiling, she took Julia by the arm. "All right, Doc, let's go find the bride now and see what she needs.

They walked around to the front of the house and found Avery and Dax under a big tree with Logan taking their picture.

"Oh good, Joy," Avery said. "We are headed to the back to take the rest of our pictures under the gazebo and then it'll be our turn. So stay close.

"Aye, aye, captain."

Avery stuck her tongue out at Joy, and both of them heard the click of Logan's camera.

"Logan!" Avery shouted. "That's gonna be horrible."

"You'd be surprised. Usually the unscripted stuff is the best." He shrugged and walked away toward the backyard.

While she'd just come from the backyard, she followed Avery and Dax back there again, Julia breaking off to find Wes so he could join them. As the backyard came into full view, she did a quick scan for Flynn and found him still on the deck, this time sitting down.

She helped Avery with her dress and bouquet, and then stepped back to watch as Logan snapped photo after photo. When it was her turn to join her sister, Dax walked away leaving them alone.

Standing next to her beautiful twin sister, who was getting married, Joy felt envious. But not in a way where she didn't want her to be happy. More in a *why can't I also be happy* way?

"So tell me," Avery said as they waited for Logan to get ready, "What did Flynn have to say about your dress?"

"Shouldn't I be asking you that?"

"Pfft. I knew Dax would love this dress. You, though, did not know how Flynn would react."

"He seemed to like it."

"That's all I get? Hello, it's my wedding day, you don't get to lie to me today."

"Are there other days that I am allowed to lie to you? Do you maybe have a list so I can put them in my calendar?"

Avery dropped her chin and pursed her lips. "Come on, Joy. What did he say?"

Giving in, she said, "It was less about what he said and more about him looking like he'd swallowed his tongue. Oh, and the partial hard-on when I rubbed up against him also let me know that I chose correctly."

"If I didn't love you so much and I didn't know how much you like Flynn, I never would have let you wear that dress to my wedding. But, since I look fucking fantastic in my own right, I can let it slide."

"You do look amazing. It's still hard for me to believe you're getting married today. This last year has been crazy."

"Crazy in a good way."

Logan moved in and started directing them. After several minutes, Dax came back, and then Wes, for some group pictures. When her job was over, she moved through the yard, back onto the deck where Flynn was still sitting and had been the whole time. Every time she'd looked up at him, he'd been staring at her.

From his staring alone, she'd say she was more than halfway primed and ready for their night together.

Wanting to talk to him, she began walking toward the deck. As she approached, he stood and came to the steps.

"Having fun?"

When she was at the bottom of the steps, she stopped and looked up. "I am actually. What about you?"

"This might be the best day I've ever spent doing nothing." His smile made her heart jump.

"It doesn't take much to make you happy does it?" She slowly went up the four steps until she was standing right in front of him. Smoothing her hand down his shirt, she looked up into his eyes. "I can probably help with that."

"I have no doubt about that." He lifted a hand, gripped her hip and pulled her closer to him. "Wanna start now?"

Sighing, she leaned her forehead against his. "You're gonna have to stop looking at me like that if you expect me to make it through this day."

"How am I looking at you?" His breath against her skin had her swallowing hard.

"Like all you can think about is fucking me."

He growled. "That is all I'm thinking about and when you talk dirty, I think about it even more."

Biting her lip, she leaned her face in even closer, their lips now only centimeters apart. "Dirty like saying that it's possible that I'm not wearing anything under this dress?"

His breath hitched and the next thing she knew, his lips crashed against hers. Right there on the deck in front of everyone, they were kissing. And she didn't care. All she wanted was more of him, more of his lips on hers.

Her hand was still between them, now gripping his shirt in her fist and his was on her hip, his fingers digging into her skin through the thin material of her dress. It felt amazing.

They pulled apart only when they heard Wes yell, "Get a room!" from across the yard. His eyes were dancing with humor.

"Why do we have friends again?"

Laughing, and needing some distance from the heat that he was putting out, she stepped back, releasing her grip on his shirt. "As annoying as they can be, they do keep things interesting."

"Hey, Flynn," Dax called out, "if you're finished harassing the maid of honor, maybe you could come on over and get your picture taken?"

"Looks like I'm up." He smoothed his shirt out with his hands. "Don't run away." His stern look told her he wasn't kidding nor was he talking about just today.

Any other day, with any other guy, she would have already been gone. But this was Flynn. And Flynn was different. She hoped.

"That kiss was hot," Melanie said as she came to stand next to her. "Flynn gets an A-plus for showmanship."

"I'm pretty sure he wasn't concerned about what it looked like."

"That's why he gets a high score. When you don't care, that comes across. Also not caring means he's in deep. As are you, my dear."

Joy rolled her eyes. "You guys all have opinions on my life, don't you?"

"It's what we do." She shrugged like it was no big deal. "You should have been around when Logan and I started out. Carly and Leah were always up in my business. Still are."

Joy turned her head to look at Mel. "Do you really think he's in deep?"

"Joy, look at him? He's been eye-fucking you all day. That is a man who wants you and only you."

She looked out across the yard and sure enough found him staring at her. "Do you think it's in bad form to have sex in my sister's bedroom on her wedding day?"

Melanie burst out laughing. "While I think she would understand, you might be better off waiting until you are alone. First times can be pretty intense."

She shivered at Mel's use of the word intense. If how she felt right now was any indication, Mel was right. But intense might not be a strong enough word.

As guests started filing into the backyard, Joy took Avery inside for a few final touch-ups. When Avery was ready, Joy went outside and told everyone. Because it was informal, there was no need for a big fuss. Joy took her place up front next to the minister where Dax was already standing and on the other side of him was Wes. A friend of a friend had volunteered to play the acoustic guitar as Avery walked down a makeshift aisle. When he began to play, everyone turned and watched as Avery emerged from the house.

Joy was overwhelmed with emotion as her twin sister made her way down onto the lawn and then toward them. Tears she couldn't control began to fall, making it incredibly hard to concentrate. When Avery reached Dax, he took her hand and kissed her cheek before they turned to face the minister.

The ceremony started and just a few lines in, Joy felt someone at her side. It was Flynn and he was handing her a tissue.

Which in turn made her cry even more.

He stayed by her side as her sister and Dax exchanged their vows and then kissed to seal them. Finally, the happy moment of them being husband and wife had arrived and cheers went up all around them.

People started moving around, everyone wanting to congratulate the new bride and groom. She stayed where she was, her hand automatically reaching back behind her for Flynn's.

In silence, he stood with her and watched as their friends and family milled around. It was enough to just be next to him, knowing that he was there and wasn't going anywhere else.

Minutes went by before he squeezed her hand in his, telling her it was time to join the crowd.

Turning her head, she looked up at him. "Thank you." She didn't say anything else as they began to walk.

She hugged and congratulated both her sister and her new brother-in-law, Dax, and then stood around and chatted with Addison and Ryan. Flynn was never far from her side, and it was a whole new feeling for her. She'd never had anyone who anticipated her needs like Flynn did. He knew when she needed space or when she just wanted to be touched. It was beyond anything she'd ever known.

And she was starting to like it.

When everyone had gotten food and settled in to eat, she decided it was time for her maid of honor speech. Avery had told her it was up to her on whether she did one, and at first she was relieved. But now, she realized that she wanted to say something.

Standing, she spoke loudly, "If I could have everyone's attention please," the guests all quieted down, and all eyes turned to her, "I think this is as good a time as any to toast my sister and her new husband." Looking down at Flynn, she gathered her strength. "I consider Avery and I to be pretty lucky. Growing up we always had each other. Now, I can't say that I was always a good sister or even an attentive one, but Avery was. When I was sad, she was always trying to cheer me up. When I did poorly in school, there she was at night helping me out, making sure I did well." She looked over to Avery. "We didn't have the easiest life but that never mattered to Avery. She stayed happy and cheerful even when there was nothing to be happy or cheerful about.

I used to joke that she could find the good in anyone or anything, but really it's not a joke. It's who she is. And I am beyond thankful that she has found her happy ending. There is no one in the world that deserves happiness more than Avery. And Dax, well what can I say about the man who has my sister's whole heart?" She looked at Dax. "Keep her happy and love her as you do now, and you and I are good." She raised her glass of wine. "Cheers to Avery and Dax!"

Everyone joined in, each shouting out and sipping their drinks. As she sat back down, Flynn reached over to take her hand in his, leaning in and kissing her cheek. "Nice speech."

It felt good to have him next to her, and even better to have him touching and kissing her with everyone watching.

"Thanks. I think it was easy since I pretty much know everyone here." The eating continued and you could hear conversation and laughter all around the yard. Avery looked radiant sitting next to Dax, who looked pretty damn happy himself.

The day couldn't have been more perfect.

When Avery and Dax stood, Joy knew that was her cue to turn on the music for their first dance. They had a great sound system outside and were just playing music from their phones. It was perfect for a backyard wedding.

Standing again, she walked up to the deck to where the phone was and started the song. It was an old country song that even she had never heard until Avery had played it for her. But after listening, Joy could see how right it was for the two of them. With the music playing they began to dance, and all eyes turned toward them to watch. Joy couldn't help but shed a tear as they danced, and when she felt strong, sturdy arms come around her waist, she leaned back into what she knew was Flynn's chest.

No words were needed as they swayed together watching Avery and Dax.

When the song ended, Avery shouted, "Now it's time to party!"

Joy smiled and as instructed, clicked on Avery's wedding playlist for the party music. People started standing and dancing, the noise level jumping up a few notches.

"Wanna dance?" Flynn said in her ear, his breath sending shivers down her spine.

"Can't we just stay like this?"

"We could, but if we dance, we get to be face-to-face. And if we're face-to-face, I get to see you smile, and maybe even kiss you."

"Okay your idea has merit. Come on." She grabbed his hand from where it had been resting on her stomach and pulled him down the stairs and onto the lawn with everyone else. The first few songs were fast ones, so they swiveled their hips, tapped their toes and shook their arms above their head like everyone else. He wasn't half bad and definitely had rhythm. It was impressive. When a slow song began to play, Flynn wasted no time taking her into his arms.

"Finally," he said.

They were both breathing heavy from the dancing, and she could feel his quick heartbeat mixed with her own, against her chest. Her fingers danced along his neck, playing with his hair at the base. His own hands rested right above her ass, his fingers moving in slow circles which was driving her insane.

"I can't remember the last time I slow danced." Talking was difficult. Hell, thinking was difficult with him touching her, but she needed something to take her mind off all the things she wanted to do with him.

"I think my last time might have been prom."

"I didn't go to either of my proms."

His eyes widened. "There is no way that you weren't asked."

"I wasn't really what you would call cool in high school," she admitted. "I was a loner who barely had any friends, let alone a boyfriend or even dates." Avery had been her only friend, and even she, sometimes, hadn't wanted to hang out with her.

Instead of pity, she saw something else in his eyes. Intrigue mixed with heat. "I will dance with you whenever you want. In fact, I think our next date should be dancing."

She loved that he wanted to give her something she'd never had, and because of that, she had no control over her next words. "I think our next date should be in my bed. Or maybe my kitchen table. I'd even be okay with a tent in the woods at this point."

He stopped moving, making her also stop. His mouth was open with his eyes not blinking as they stared down at her. Then, in a move she'd never forget, he lifted her off her feet, at the same time as his lips came down on hers.

Her feet dangled in the air as he, literally, took her breath away with the kiss. The feeling of being completely in his control was thrilling. When she again felt the ground under her, she wasn't ready to let him go, or for the kiss to end. So she gripped his hair in her fingers and tugged him even closer. The way he made her feel, the way he felt up against her, there was no way she was ready for that to end.

She was so enthralled in their kiss, that even when she heard Carly's voice directly behind her say, "I've never been into voyeurism, but if you insist on fucking right here on the lawn, I think we can all agree that we'd watch," she continued to hold tight to Flynn.

His lips left hers but his grip never loosened. His eyes met hers making her practically drown in the depths of the emotion. "I think that's our cue to get out of here."

She wanted to. In fact, there was nothing she could ever remember wanting more. But it was her sister's wedding day. Leaving early was a dick move. And while she'd been a dick for a lot of her life, she wasn't anymore.

"I can't." Before she could explain though, Avery walked up next to them.

"You can and you will. Go, Joy. Live life to the fullest and don't ever let anything, me included, hold you back."

Letting go of Flynn, she turned to her sister. "Are you sure? I don't mind staying. There's a lot to clean up."

Avery waved her off. "Dax's mom has offered to stay and clean up. It was her gift to us." She pulled Joy in for a hug. "I found my happiness, now go and find yours," Avery whispered into her ear.

Joy swallowed as she pulled back. She didn't know if Flynn was her happy, as Avery had put it, but she was definitely willing to try to find out. "Congrats again. Have a great honeymoon."

When Avery walked away, Joy reached out and took Flynn's hand. "Looks like we got the go ahead to get out of here. Still interested?"

"I'm pretty sure my interest is still completely visible under my pants."

His words had her looking south to where, sure enough, there was a rather large bulge. Sucking her bottom lip into her mouth, she slowly lifted her eyes back to his. Somehow the heat they'd held only moments earlier had intensified. Swallowing, she opened her mouth to speak, but no words seemed to come.

And then, in another move that she will never forget, Flynn bent down low and basically threw her over his shoulder. She squealed, all eyes immediately turning toward them. And because she was in a dress, she used her hands to make sure all her private parts weren't out for the whole world to see.

She heard catcalls, whistles and one "It's about time!" as Flynn strode toward the front of the house. "Put me down, you big buffoon." She swatted his back, pretending to be annoyed. In reality, she was exponentially turned on. His caveman act was hot as fuck.

Who knew?

His footsteps slowed and in an instant she was planted back on her feet, his truck against her back. "Get in the truck, Joy." It wasn't a question. It was a demand.

Running her hands up his chest, she asked, "What if I don't want to?"

His own hands gripped hers pulling them away from his body. "Don't. I have zero willpower right now. If you touch me, we won't make it to my house." He lifted an eyebrow at her. "And believe me, you want to make it to my house."

His words held so much innuendo and promise for what would happen once they were at his house. And, because she wanted all the same things he did, she turned and got inside the truck. He closed the door and quickly ran around the front of the truck. She took several deep breaths to try to control her emotions. Emotions that were running wild wondering if she was doing the right thing. But, when he slid into the truck and turned to smile at her, she knew she was.

Flynn was absolutely her happy place.

Chapter 12

Flynn wasn't sure how he didn't crash as he drove to his house. The smell of Joy alone had him so hard that he was positive he was going to come in his pants. Add to that her soft breathing and her eyes that he could feel looking at him and he was a goner.

"Do me a favor and don't look at me." He didn't dare glance over to her as he said the words.

A soft chuckle escaped her. "So now I can't touch you or look at you? Do you have superpowers or something? How is sex going to work without those two things?"

"You can do both of those and more, just not until we are at my house."

"You're that out of control?"

Finally he looked at her. "No, you just have that much power."

He turned back to watch the road as seconds of silence ticked by. When he looked at her again, an evil grin appeared on her face.

Then she did the unthinkable.

Touched his thigh.

His breathing hitched and he felt himself tense under her palm. "Joy." His voice was rough, the words barely audible.

"Flynn," she said, mocking him. "I like touching you. It gives me strength. So that power I have over you, is really because of you, if you think about it."

Thinking and reasoning, while she was touching him, was not easy to do. Pushing through the sex thoughts that filled his brain, he kept driving while her hand moved higher and higher on his leg. He wasn't sure how he was breathing let alone driving, but somehow he pulled into his driveway, slammed the car into park and pulled Joy across the seat.

"Put your hands on me now," she said as she tried to settle down onto his lap. "Right now."

Already there, he scrunched her dress up and around her waist and immediately noticed she was completely bare underneath. His hands stilled. Sure, she'd mentioned it, but knowing and feeling, were two very different things.

"No underwear might be the best thing ever."

With a smile, she fully settled on top of him. "I didn't want any lines." She leaned into his ear. "And I wanted to surprise you."

"Oh, you definitely surprised me." His hands began to once again move, and soon he was clutching her bare ass in both hands. "This is crazy. We could be inside, in a bed, or on a couch."

"Or up against a wall," she helped him out.

"Yeah or that. But instead we are in my driveway, in my truck."

Her fingers were tickling the skin at the back of his neck. "We'll get there. But first I need you to kiss me. Kiss me like your life depends on it."

"I'm pretty sure it does," he said, as he tilted his face up and took her lips with his own. Her lips against his were swift and electric. Not that he minded, but this was not a woman who wanted to go slow. His hands moved of their own free will up her back and then down again to grab and hold onto her glorious ass. Her arms were tight around his neck making it so there was no room between their bodies.

You couldn't even slip a piece of paper between them.

She whimpered when his fingers began to explore lower and when he felt her wetness between her legs, he whimpered right along with her.

He had a feeling that Joy's pussy could bring him to his knees. Literally.

And he didn't think he'd mind one bit.

He in no way wanted to stop kissing and touching her but he also wanted to see her. And he couldn't do that in the driver's seat of his truck.

Finding the handle, he pulled on it until his door opened. Laughing as they went, he dragged her with him out of the truck and slammed the door. She was lowering her dress as she laughed and on unsteady legs began walking up his driveway.

"I like your house."

It wasn't special or fancy, but it was his, and he loved it. He'd only bought it two years ago and spent most of that time remodeling the inside. He was finally finished though and had been dying for Joy to see it.

She would be the first.

Even his brother hadn't been there since he'd finished all the work.

Tapping in the code to the garage, he wrapped his arm around Joy's waist as they waited for it to open.

"How long have you lived here?"

"About two years."

Once the garage was open, he guided her inside the garage and then up the steps and into the house. Hitting the button to close the garage, he also flipped the switch on the wall of the kitchen to turn on the lights.

"Wow," Joy said and stepped further into his house. "This is fantastic." She ran her hand over the marble countertop of his small island. "From the outside you'd never know that it was all brand new in here."

"Yeah, I liked the older look outside so I left it. But in here, I wanted it to be functional and livable."

She turned back to face him. "While I'd love to see the rest," she took a step toward him, "right now there's something else I want more."

Grabbing her hand, he pulled her up against him. "Is that right?"

"Oh yeah." She ground her hips against his, making him groan and start walking her backward. He didn't kiss her as they moved through his house, but he did use his hands to feel every one of her curves under her dress.

His house was two stories, but the master bedroom was on the first floor, making it easy to maneuver them directly into it. Before he pushed her back on the bed, he gathered the material of her dress in his hands, lifting it up and over her head.

He was rewarded with finding her completely naked underneath.

"Fuck, you're gorgeous." He wanted to put his mouth and hands everywhere, but didn't know where to start.

"Your turn," she said and instead of unbuttoning his shirt, she gripped it in her hands and ripped it off.

He'd never been more turned on.

"That's better," she said as her fingers danced over his chest and ribcage. They went even lower but before they could reach the button on his pants, he stopped her.

"Let's leave these on for now." If his pants came off, this would be the shortest lovemaking in history.

Toeing his shoes off, he started kissing her neck, all the while his hands caressing her skin. Under his hands she was soft and silky, making it easy to slide his hands down her body.

"You're moving too slow, Flynn. I need more." Her husky voice demanding he move faster.

Pushing her down the bed, he followed and landed on top of her. "I wanted this first time to be more." He'd wanted it to be perfect.

She smoothed his hair back with her hand. "Stop worrying about what you think I need and take what you want. I'm pretty sure I want the same thing." She pulled his face closer, taking his lips with hers. "We can go slow the second time. Or maybe the third."

Her words, and how well she seemed to know that he was trying to go slow for her, spurred him on. There was no more slow. He growled as he took her mouth and his hands began to furiously touch every part of her he could reach.

She was moaning at his every touch along with doing some touching of her own. It seemed like her hands were everywhere and that only made him move faster. He felt like he'd been waiting for this moment his whole life.

The moment where dream became reality.

It was...well, it was pure joy.

Her name fit well for what he felt when they were together.

And he never wanted it to end.

Moving from her mouth, he trailed his kisses to her neck and eventually to her breasts. Oh man, her breasts were a thing of beauty. Firm, round and the perfect size to fit in his palm. Her breath hitched when he ran his tongue over the tip of one, letting him know she was sensitive to the touch. But when she arched her back and pushed herself further into his mouth, he realized sensitivity might not be a bad thing.

Her skin tasted of summer and fresh berries as he continued to lap at her breasts. Her hands were now in his hair, gripping and urging him on. Turning his head to the side, he rubbed his beard over one nipple. That had her pulling even harder on his hair.

"Holy shit! Do that again."

He did and this time she was writhing under him. He wasn't positive, but he swore she was on the verge of orgasm. The thought of that made him do it again and this time, she did come.

Loudly.

Screaming his name.

It was the best fucking sound in the world.

"What the hell," she said when he lifted his head and looked up at her.

"Seems like you really liked what I was doing."

"I've never...that hasn't...I didn't know I could. Not from that alone."

He smiled and kissed her lips. "It was a first for me too."

"Can we maybe move this along?" She ran her fingers through his beard. "Now that I'm feeling relaxed, I want more." Her other hand trailed down his body until it gripped his ass and pulled him in tighter to her, his erection nestled right where it wanted to be.

"I think I can accommodate that request." He sat up, unbuttoned his pants and slid them down his legs along with his boxers, then kicked them the rest of the way off. As he started to lie back on top of her, she stopped him.

"I should have known." When he looked at her, he saw that she was looking at his dick.

"Something wrong?"

"Seriously, you are not only hot and sexy and built like a fucking God, but you also have a huge dick. Other guys must hate you."

Laughing, he lowered himself on top of her, kissing her shoulder. "As far as I know, no guys have seen my dick."

Scoffing, she dropped her head back to give him better access. "Believe me, guys have looked. If you were standing next to them in a restroom, they wanted to know what you were packing."

"Know a lot about men's restrooms, do ya?" He was now at her ribs, sliding lower every second.

"I just know guys. And they would want to know if they measured up."

Shaking his head against her stomach, he continued his journey. As he moved between her legs, he made sure not to touch her already slick pussy. But he did look, and it had him panting for a taste. Starting at her knee, he ran a bearded cheek up one side of her leg.

"Oh God, yes."

Smiling he did it again to the other side, her response was virtually the same. Ready to put them both out of their misery, he zeroed in on his target and licked right up her center.

Her taste was beyond what he'd expected and now that he'd touched her, he needed more. He ate at her as her juices covered his face and beard. She moved under him with total abandon as his mouth worked to please her. He loved how free she was with her body and how much she seemed to love what he was doing to her. Wrapping his teeth around her clit, he bit down lightly, then soothed it with his tongue. She screamed out and tightened her legs around his head.

Never had a woman been so easy to please.

He lapped up her juices as she came down from her high before sitting back between her legs. Her skin was flushed all over and she had a lazy smile on her lips.

"Did you, like, take classes or something?"

He stood, laughing as he moved to his nightstand to grab a condom. "A class in eating pussy. That would be interesting."

"It's the only way I can think to explain how well you make me come." She watched intently as he rolled the condom down his enlarged cock.

"Maybe it's just us." He knelt on the bed between her legs. "It's possible that, class or not, I'm the only one who will ever be able to make you come like that."

Her eyes were still on his cock and he moved closer and closer to her body. "That might be true." She swallowed and looked up at him. "I'm nervous."

He stopped moving. "Nervous. Why?"

"This is you. Us. I don't want to ruin this."

"You aren't going to ruin this." He leaned down, kissing her on the lips. "Nothing can ruin this." Lining himself up, inch by inch, he began sliding inside her tight heat. It was glorious, and the most magnificent feeling he'd ever experienced.

Settled deeply inside her, he slowly began to move. Her body seemed to be in tune with his own and moved in perfect rhythm. She held his gaze as they made love and he never wanted the moment to end.

He felt her arms go around his body and then felt her fingernails dig into his skin right above his ass. If that wasn't the international signal to go faster, he wasn't sure what was.

His pace picked up and soon he was thrusting deep inside her body. So deep and so hard that his mattress started squeaking. He saw her smile at the noise and felt his own smile turn up his lips..

Who knew sex could be so much fun?

Sealing his lips with hers, he shortened his strokes and felt her quiver under him. When her pussy gripped him tighter and she moaned into his mouth, he knew she was coming and let himself go over with her.

It was quite possibly the best first time ever, not to mention, the best anytime ever.

"Am I still alive?"

She was still under him, her eyes closed.

"If you're speaking I assume you are alive."

She opened her eyes. "This isn't the time for reasoning."

He bent, rubbing his beard along her cheek before kissing her lips one last time. Lifting up to his arms, he carefully pulled out of her warm heat and stood. After a quick trip to the bathroom to dispose of the condom and get a warm washcloth for Joy, he returned and started to clean her up.

"Wh–" she stuttered when the warm cloth touched her most intimate place. "What are you doing?"

Her expression told him that no one had ever taken care of her before. That was a shame. Bending over her on the bed, he used his free hand to caress her face. "Just lie there and relax. It gives me pleasure to take care of you."

It took a second, but her face relaxed. He returned the washcloth to his bathroom before climbing back in bed with her and gathering her in his arms.

"Hey Flynn," she said as she rested her head on his chest. "It was okay, right?"

He looked down at her. "Are you seriously asking if it was good for me?"

When she flicked her eyes up to his, he saw the fear. "I just wasn't sure."

"Joy, it was fucking magnificent. It was everything I ever wanted and then some."

The fear disappeared, only to be replaced by disbelief. "But you did all the work."

Laughing he pulled her back to him and kissed her head. "Silly women. Pleasure comes in all forms, and giving it to you, seeing your face and how much you are enjoying yourself, that is a huge turn-on for me."

"Well, then you must still be turned on, because I have never felt anything close to that."

"Haven't you learned by now...I'm always turned on around and by you."

Lazily her fingers started to draw circles on his bare chest. "I can't believe I left my sister's wedding to go have sex. God, I'm a horrible human being."

"On the contrary. A horrible human being would have left without her sister's permission. But in your case, you had it."

"So you're saying I should stop worrying about it?"

He rolled her over so she was on top of him, running his hands up her sides. "That's exactly what I am saying. Plus, I am sure we can find something better to do that makes you stop thinking."

Her legs slid up his until she was sitting on top of him, his cock nestled against her warm heat. "I think it's only fair of me to even things up a little." Before he could reach for her and tell her he didn't need things evened up, she was already down between his legs, her mouth perilously close to his dick. Slowly she moved her hand up and down his shaft. "This is some pretty impressive recuperating power."

More than ready to watch the show she was about to put on, he crossed his arms under his head. "That's all you."

"Then I guess I should help you out." With a sly smile, she closed the distance between her mouth and his cock, licking the head.

He wasn't sure how he didn't move or grab her head and shove it on his cock. But somehow, he remained where he was. When her tongue licked him again though, his cock jumped in her hand.

Lifting her eyes to his, she smirked. "Someone likes that."

"Umm yeah, he's definitely not complaining."

"I wonder if you would like this too." She'd barely finished her words when her whole mouth engulfed him.

His hips lifted of their own accord making her take him even deeper. But she didn't seem to mind. In fact, her next downward stroke she somehow took him all the way in, the head hitting the back of her throat. He was shocked, turned on, and about to come all at the same time. She kept on sucking him off, alternating between shallow and deep. It wasn't long before he was panting heavily and on the verge of orgasm. Then she took him deep once more and when he hit the back of her throat, she swallowed.

That was it.

He couldn't hold back another second.

He came fast and furious, her eyes lifted to his, watching him the whole time she accepted his release and then swallowed it all down.

His already spent dick twitched at the sight.

Damn this fucking amazing women.

Chapter 13

Flynn was a God.

A fucking sex God who knew her body like he knew the back of his own hand.

She was starting to wonder if all the sex she'd had in her life could even be called sex. It wasn't in the same stratosphere as what she and Flynn had just done.

If everything she'd ever thought about sex was wrong, maybe it was the same with other things in life.

Was chocolate really the best ice cream flavor? Maybe vanilla wasn't as vanilla as she'd always thought.

She and Flynn had been lounging in bed for the last few minutes, but unlike every other time in her life where sex had made her tired, she was energized.

"Flynn," she yanked on his arm, "show me the rest of your house."

Looking back she caught him yawning. "Aren't you tired?"

"It's only eight o'clock. Plus someone," she raised her eyebrow, "gave me all this energy."

Shaking his head, he sat up. "Apparently I didn't do a good enough job wearing you out."

He looked so cute with his hair rumpled and his beard sticking out in all directions. "You did more than enough. I just have all this energy," she shook her hands in the air, "and I really want to see your house."

"All right, crazy. Come on." He stepped out of bed grabbing a pair of shorts from a nearby chair. She practically jumped off the bed, and because she had nothing but her dress to wear, she grabbed his white button down that he'd been wearing. Then she remembered that she'd ripped it off him and the buttons were gone.

"Need something to wear?" He was standing at the foot of the bed, a smirk on his face.

Tilting her head to the side, she held up his ruined shirt. "Sorry about this."

He stepped forward, grabbing it from her hand and pulling her toward him. "I'm keeping it as a memento of the best night of my life."

Looking up at him, she saw the truth of his words in his eyes. "Mine too."

What felt like minutes passed, when in reality it was probably just a few seconds before he stepped back. Grabbing a t-shirt off the same chair he'd gotten his shorts, he threw it to her. "Put this on or I won't be responsible for my actions."

"You know, if you'd given me a few minutes before we left the wedding, I could have grabbed the bag I'd packed from my car. Then I wouldn't have to be pantyless all night."

He stepped toward her again, this time reaching around to grab her bare ass. "I like you pantyless." His lips touched hers in a sensual kiss that had her reaching for him so she could hold on to something. Ending the kiss abruptly, he dropped his forehead to hers. "Although, I can see how it could be a distraction."

Slapping the side of his arm, she pushed away from his body. "Stop stalling and show me your house."

Taking her hand, which she secretly loved, he started to lead her out of the room but then stopped. "I guess I should start with my bathroom, since we're here." Backtracking, they walked several feet, entering the bathroom.

And what a bathroom it was. Huge tub with tile all around it and steps leading up to it. Dual sinks, a shower with glass walls all around and a separate room for the actual bathroom.

"This is..." Really she had no words. It was spectacular.

"And my mom wins again."

She looked over to him, frowning. "Why your mom?"

"Because she told me that the master bath had to be grand. Her words. If it had been up to me, I would have made it fairly plain with just a shower. I've never even used that tub."

She knew her mouth was hanging open at his admission. "You're insane. If this was mine, I'd use it every day."

"Then consider it yours."

She wasn't sure what to say to that or how to respond. So instead she ignored it. "Tell your mom that she was most definitely right. This bathroom is a work of art."

From there he showed her the guest bedroom, his office, the living room and the kitchen which she'd already seen. The only thing he didn't show her was the basement and that was because it was unfinished. He had plans to finish it but it was last on his list.

"I'll get to it, eventually."

"It's really a great house, Flynn." She was a little envious of everything he had. Sure, she was several years younger, but really, if you looked at it, she had nothing to show for those years.

He looked around as if seeing it from her eyes and shrugged. "I like it."

Smiling, she moved in front of him jumping up onto the counter, using her legs to pull him into her body. "Have you ever done anything...wicked on this counter?"

His hands glided up her legs, finally resting on her waist. "I've never done anything wicked, or otherwise, anywhere in this house." He nipped at her lower lip with his teeth. "Just you."

"Now I know that's a lie." When he started to speak, she shushed him up with a quick kiss. "There's no way you haven't jerked off in your bed."

His eyes widened his head tilting to the side. "Pictured that, have you?"

"So. Many. Times."

His hands moved higher, up under his t-shirt she was wearing, until each of his hands was cupping a breast. "For the last six months, every time I touched myself, you were right there with me. In my head, where my hands would run over your imaginary curves and my mouth licked your imaginary pussy." His fingers were plucking at her already erect nipples. "You starred in every fantasy I had. But now I don't have to wonder. Now I get to touch and taste you all I want."

She thought he'd kiss her then, but instead, his mouth latched on to her neck and teased and tasted until she was dying for more. Her own arms snaked between them where she found him already rock hard, a drop of moisture covering the head of his cock.

Groaning, he bit down on her neck. She knew there would be a mark there and couldn't wait to see it. And maybe even have others see it.

She was a freak.

"Joy, baby, are you sore?" he asked as one of his hands skated down her stomach.

She wanted to say no because she wanted him so much. But she was sore. Incredibly so. Leaning back, she groaned. "I just started something that we can't finish, didn't I?"

His hands stilled as his head came up to meet her hers. "I'm pretty sure we are both at fault."

Biting her bottom lip, she lowered her legs from around his body and slipped off the counter.

"Would you like to take a bath?"

She looked up at him and smiled. "I'd love to take a bath."

"Go ahead then and when you get out, I'll have some food ready."

"You're not going to join me?"

"The whole point of the bath is to help the soreness. If I was in there with you, we would only be making it worse."

He made a good point.

She took a long bath and when she got out, they ate from a tray he'd made up of fruit, cheese and crackers, and chips and salsa while they sat on the couch watching a movie. After a few hours, she was starting to doze off when Flynn shut off the television.

"Come on, sleepyhead, let's get to bed."

She was shocked when he picked her up and strode down the hall to his bedroom.

"What is your deal with carrying me?" she asked sleepily.

"I like the way you feel in my arms. You can't fault me for that."

As she snuggled in closer to him, she was starting to think that she also liked the way she felt in his arms.

Lowering her to the bed, she watched as he shed his shorts, and slid in next to her. Wrapping his arms around her, he tucked her into his side and kissed the top of her head. "Good night, my sweet, Joy."

She murmured "Good night" and then drifted off to possibly her best night's sleep ever.

The next time she opened her eyes, she thought for sure she was dreaming. She'd had this dream many times, so she knew it well. Flynn with his head between her legs, lapping at her pussy.

Only this was no dream.

It was one hundred percent real and she was one hundred percent on the verge of orgasm.

"Flynn," she moaned, stretching her arms above her head and looking down to where his head was between her legs.

His eyes lifted up to hers, a glint in them as he continued his slow assault on her pussy. And slow it was. His movements weren't hurried or fast, instead he was licking her at a slow pace, almost like he was savoring every minute of it.

She wasn't complaining though.

It might just be her new favorite way to wake up.

When her orgasm finally came, it was like nothing she'd ever experienced before. It felt like one long wave of mini quakes rolling through her body. And it went on and on and on with him continuing to slowly lap at her. Finally, she had to pull him up to her, just to make him stop.

"Enough," she sighed. "I can't take anymore."

He was lying on top of her, his beard coated with her juices.

Hmm, maybe she could take more.

"I could do that forever."

His eyes held the truth that he spoke and Joy wondered—not for the first time—why she had resisted him for so long. "You're a strange man, Flynn."

"Takes one to know one." He kissed her lips, Joy easily tasting herself on his mouth, before he rolled off to the side of the bed.

Closing her eyes, she let feelings that she never thought she'd have, rush over her. Flynn didn't treat her like a fragile woman who needed his help, nor did he beat around the bush when they talked. She felt like she owed him the same.

"Were you for real when you said you were halfway in love with me?" Opening her eyes, she turned her head to the side to meet Flynn's gaze.

"I'm not sure how to answer that."

"So it wasn't true?" She turned fully on her side, tucking her hand under her head.

"It was true, but only half true." He also turned onto his side, one of his hands reaching out to push hair off her face.

"I don't think I understand what that means."

"I'm more than halfway in love with you, Joy, but I'm afraid you aren't ready and I don't want to push you."

She swallowed the happiness that had formed. He was in love with her. All the way in love with her.

Had anyone ever loved her? She wasn't sure. Well other than Avery. But that wasn't the same. Some days she wasn't even sure her mom or dad loved her the way a parent was supposed to love a child. They loved her because they had to, not because they felt an all consuming need to.

Reaching out a hand, she pulled herself closer to Flynn, until they were nose-to-nose. "A few days ago, if you had said that to me, I would have run out of this house so fast that there would be a Joy shaped hole in your wall. But today," she shrugged the best she could while lying down, "While I can't say it back, yet, it doesn't make me want to run away. In fact, I might even want to run full steam ahead."

A smile lit up his face. "I can live with that. And I'll do everything I can not to rush you. All I want is to be with you."

"I want to be with you too."

For several long minutes they stayed in bed, facing each other, just enjoying being next to each other. Finally, when her stomach rumbled and Flynn laughed, they got up. He made himself some coffee while she chose water and rummaged through his fridge for something to eat. Deciding on eggs, she offered to cook while he took a shower.

What she really wanted was to take a shower with him, but that would lead to more sexual explorations, and while that was great, her body really needed a break.

After breakfast, and because they both had the day off, they joined Mel and Logan for a day out on the water.

Flynn didn't have his own boat, but Logan did and had no problem sharing it with them.

"You left awfully early last night," Mel said, when it was just the two of them sitting in the back of the boat while the guys carried down coolers and supplies.

"With permission from the bride."

"I heard about that and we all saw that movie worthy kiss that Flynn planted on you." She fanned herself. "Logan has moves, but

Flynn has just put the guys on blast. They're gonna have to step up their game."

Joy laughed. "I don't think any of the guys in this town are in trouble of not being romantic. We live in a freaking romance novel."

"Am I gonna get details or are you gonna keep them all to yourself?"

"I'm not so sure I should kiss and tell."

"Listen you're fairly new here so you might not know the rules, but you are required to kiss and tell. It's in the friendship bylaws."

Joy lifted her sunglasses and glared at Mel. "You guys are all insane. I might need to rethink living in this town."

"Pfft," Mel waved her comment off, "there is no place better than Cedarville so don't even try. Now give me the details before the guys get back on this boat."

Shaking her head, Joy gave in. "I've had a lot of sex, but Flynn, he blew my mind. Literally. I had no idea it could be that way. Nor did I know that a guy could love pleasuring me more than getting his own pleasure."

"Ah yeah, I know all about that. Logan would gladly go down on me for hours without wanting anything in return."

"So this is a normal thing?"

"I don't think it's normal, but I think when a guy is in love, he gets just as much out of giving pleasure as he does from getting."

"I guess that makes sense. I mean I think I would gladly give him a blow job without expecting anything else."

"Are you saying you're in love with Flynn?"

Oh hell, she'd really walked right into that one. "Maybe, I don't know." She hung her head. "Probably." It was time to start being honest. "He's not like anyone I've ever known. When I look at him, all I want is to be with him. He makes me happy."

"Yeah, I know that feeling." She had a wistful look on her face. "Logan and I had been friends since we were kids and I'd loved him forever. Looking at him and not being able to be with him, made my heart hurt, but it also made me happy to just be around him."

"You are perfect for each other. I can't imagine either one of you with anyone else."

"It took us a long time to get to where we are and it didn't happen overnight. The best advice I can give you is to be honest with each other, and don't worry if things move too fast or too slow. Time is irrelevant when it comes to love."

Be honest. That was hard for her. She was used to being someone she wasn't but still that morning she'd been completely honest with Flynn and told him that she wasn't where he was —more than halfway in love—but that she wasn't afraid of going there.

That was a huge step for her.

She was done with being afraid, with being unhappy. She wanted happiness for herself in all aspects of her life. And Flynn made her happy.

That was part of what scared her though.

She didn't want her happiness to be so reliant on another person.

People inevitably let you down.

Chapter 14

He'd had enough.

Enough of sleeping without her.

Enough of her excuses.

He'd taken her home Sunday after their day on the lake, after dinner, and after sex. She'd said she really needed to get home to readjust for her work week.

That was bullshit.

At least Flynn had thought it was bullshit.

He'd wanted her to stay.

He'd wanted to beg her to stay.

But he wasn't an idiot and he knew she needed more time.

Now though, it was Tuesday, and again she was saying she was too busy, too tired to see him. But he wasn't having it. Parking outside her building, he took several deep breaths before finally opening the door.

He wasn't sure if he was doing the right thing, but if there was one thing his parents had taught him growing up, it was to never give up on your dreams.

Joy was his dream.

With a heavy hand, he knocked on her door. Seconds ticked by before it flew open.

"Thank God." She gripped the front of his shirt and pulled him into her apartment. Before he could speak or even wrap his mind about what was happening, she was glued to him, her lips devouring his.

He wasn't one to question anything that put her in his arms, but he needed to know what was happening.

"Joy," he murmured, pulling away from her.

"Oh God, I've ruined it haven't I?" she covered her face with her hand and walked away.

"Joy," he said again, following her. Reaching out, he gripped her elbow and turned her back to face him. "What's going on?"

"I was trying to see if I could be without you and still be happy."

He frowned. "What are you talking about?"

"I didn't want my happiness to be defined by you. I wanted to know that I could be happy without you."

Closing his eyes, he shook his head, a small laugh escaping. "You crazy, insane, lunatic of a woman." He pulled her to him, enveloping her in his arms. "Why do you care where the happiness comes from? If something makes you happy you keep doing it. You don't throw it away."

"I don't like relying on anyone. I wanted to be happy because I did it. Not because of you."

"Having people in your life that make you happy doesn't make you weak. It makes you pretty fucking smart for choosing the right people." He kissed the top of her head. "You make me happy and you don't see me pushing you away."

She looked up at him through glassy eyes. "I'm so bad at this. Why do you even like me?"

"Because just talking to you or holding you, even when you're being stupid, makes my whole day better. I've been a miserable ass for two days. Just ask my guys. I think a few of them were ready to quit and how the hell would I have explained that to Dax."

"You were really miserable?"

Resting his forehead against hers, he said, "Yeah, it was the worst two days of my life."

Her small fingers lifted and began to play with his beard. "Mine too. Before you knocked on my door, I was debating with myself about coming to see you. I just wasn't sure if you'd want to see me."

"You never have to wonder about that. I always want to see you. Or talk to you. You don't need to hold yourself back from me. Ever."

Her eyes searched his. "Can you stay?" She shook her head. "Let me rephrase that. I'd really like you to stay if you can."

Smiling, he kissed the tip of her nose. "I'd love to stay."

"Have you eaten? I can make us some dinner?" As she talked, he was slowly pushing her backward.

"There's only one thing I want in my mouth right now." Her eyes widened and then she smiled.

"Me first." And without another word, she sank to her knees right there in her living room. For a second he thought he might have a stroke.

"Joy." He gripped her hair, probably a little too tight. "You don't have to."

She had his pants undone and his cock already out. "I want to. I really, really want to." As she spoke she was stroking him up and down, making him harder with each stroke.

His breath hitched as he watched her take him into her mouth. Blow jobs had always been one of those things that he was fine with, but he didn't need. It was mainly because all the women he'd been with never loved doing it. Joy though, she sucked his cock with gusto, almost like she had to have it.

And that was a huge fucking turn on.

Her mouth was warm and her tongue teased the underside easily. He was torn between pulling her off and burying himself deep inside her tight pussy, or letting her finish and watching her swallow down his release.

Such a hard decision.

In the end, her pussy won.

Yanking her up and off him, he kicked off his shorts at the same time as he stripped her of her own. Bending over he quickly found his wallet and the condom he'd put in there earlier. Without words, he pulled her up against him and kissed her hard before turning her and bending her over the arm of the couch. He rolled the condom on, her head turning to watch him.

He was crazy to have her and a little afraid he might hurt her in the process. "This isn't going to be slow. I need you too much."

"Give me everything you've got."

He took her at her word, slamming his cock deep into her in one thrust. She was so tight, so warm, that as much as he wanted this to last, it probably wouldn't. He fucked her with wild abandon, something he wasn't sure he'd ever done before with any other woman. This kind of deep, intense, soul wrenching fuck, was only something you could do if you loved that person.

Sure that sounded ass backward, but to Flynn it was true.

And he loved Joy with everything he had.

He hoped that came through with what they were doing

Her moans and screams had him right on the edge, and thankfully, before he could find his own release, she squeezed his cock tight and came hard. He loved the feel of pumping into her when she was gripping and pulsing around him. It was the final straw, and with a loud groan that he hoped like hell her neighbors didn't hear, he came.

Her body was limp under his and she sagged even further into the couch.

"Mother of God, Flynn, are you trying to kill me?"

Alarmed that maybe he'd hurt her, he stood to his full height and quickly pulled out. "Oh shit, Joy, I'm so sorry. I got carried away."

Looking back over her shoulder, she scowled. "What are you talking about? Why would you be sorry?"

"Because I hurt you." He wanted to drop to his knees and beg her not to hold this against him. He'd promise to never again treat her like anything but the finest china.

"Flynn, you didn't hurt me. Well, maybe you gave me a bruise or two on my hips from where your fingers were digging into my skin, but I like that. Hell, I liked it all." Standing up, she turned to face him. "When I asked if you were trying to kill me, I meant sexually."

"Oh." His mouth dropped open. She sounded like she'd liked it, meaning he hadn't done anything wrong.

"Relax, Flynn. If I hadn't liked what we were doing, I would have spoken up." She stood up on her tiptoes and kissed him.

"I would never hurt you." He needed her to know that.

"I'm stupid about a lot of things, but that is not one of them. I know without a doubt that you wouldn't do anything that I didn't like."

Because he couldn't stand there with his dick still out and her only half dressed and not want her, he made a quick bathroom run and dressed. When he came back out, she was also dressed, only now she was in the kitchen.

"How does spaghetti sound?"

"Perfect." he walked behind her, his body aligning with hers and kissed her neck. "It sounds just perfect."

He felt her shiver under him. "Go away if you want to eat." She turned in his arms. "I can't think with you touching me."

"My problem is the exact opposite. I think better when I can touch you."

Shaking her head, she pushed him away. "Grab a beer, turn on some ESPN, and relax."

Laughing, he did as she asked. Kinda. For fifteen minutes he sat on the couch and pretended to watch TV when in reality, he was watching her. She moved fluidly around the small kitchen, easily making their meal. Even cooking, she was sexy.

He'd probably find her sexy if she was digging in the mud.

Taking a sip of his beer, he tried to stop looking at her. But it was impossible. She was gorgeous. And all his.

That was the part he loved.

"Come and get it!" she shouted, making him laugh.

"Smells good." He took a seat at her small table where the food was already plated and ready for them.

"It's just spaghetti. Nothing fancy."

She said it in a way that he could tell she was putting herself down. And that wasn't acceptable. "It's better than I can do. Mom tried to teach me to cook but I was useless in the kitchen. I can burn water. Wyatt though, he loved it. Sometimes, he gets the urge to cook and I let him come feed me."

"No one ever really taught me and I never really had the desire to learn. I always figured I could just eat out or buy pre-made stuff."

"That's how I feel, which is why you see me at Dockside so much." He took a bite making sure she could see on his face how much he liked it. He didn't care that it came from a jar or that it was only spaghetti. It was her doing something for him that counted. "Tell me about your day?"

They talked as they ate, her telling him about a few of her clients and him talking about one of his projects that was an old home that was being restored. As they were cleaning up the dishes, a knock sounded on the door. When she opened it, Flynn saw his brother standing there.

"Wyatt, what are you doing here?"

He inclined his head. "I could ask you the same thing."

"I'm having dinner with my girlfriend." He was standing close enough to Joy that he saw how the words made her stiffen. Stepping forward, he reached out for her hand to try to ease her shock.

She was his girlfriend, even if hearing the words made her freak.

"Interesting turn of events."

"Would you like to come in?" Joy offered.

"I don't want to bother you guys. I just came by to check on the air conditioning and make sure everything was working okay."

"You might as well come in," Flynn said.

"Please stay for a minute," Joy added. "When I first met you I had no idea you were Flynn's brother, and now that I do, I'd like to get to know you."

He smiled, one of his big goofy smiles, and walked into the apartment. "I'm guessing I don't need to ask about the A/C unit as Flynn probably has that under control."

Joy looked up at Flynn. "It hasn't been discussed much, but I'm pretty sure he would fix it if I asked him to."

Leaning down, he kissed her lightly saying, "I'll fix anything you need fixed."

"Holy crap," Wyatt practically shouted. "This is for real." He waved his hand between Flynn and Joy. "I've never in my life seen Flynn voluntarily kiss a woman in front of me."

"This is most definitely for real, little brother." Flynn sat on the couch, Joy tucked in next to him. "What's going on with you?"

"Oh no, you don't get off that easily. Mom is gonna grill me about this, and I want to have some information for her."

Flynn rolled his eyes. "Mom already knows about Joy."

"What?" Joy screeched looking up at him. "How is that possible?"

Oops. Maybe he should have kept that tidbit of info to himself. Too late now. "She kept asking me why I wasn't dating and because lying to my mom just isn't something you do," he looked to Wyatt for clarification on that and he nodded, "I told her I'd met someone who I really liked, but that she, meaning you, wasn't ready yet for what I was."

"Oh great, so now your mom hates me and she's never even met me." She flopped back against the couch.

Thankfully, Wyatt chimed in. "If anything, she probably likes you more, because you didn't give into Flynn's charms immediately. She's not a fan of weak women who don't know their own minds."

"Wyatt's not wrong. Plus, there's the story of how she and dad met."

"Oh I forgot about that," Wyatt said. "Oh, she's really going to like you."

"Can someone please enlighten me?"

"Mom and dad met while in their senior year of college. But, mom wanted nothing to do with dad, mainly because she was focused on her studies and she thought he was a pretty boy. But, for months, dad would just be where she was, letting her see him around, to get used to him. Until one day, she needed something and he just so happened to be there. That day sealed the deal for them because it was then that mom realized having someone around who she could count on, who would always be there, wasn't such a bad thing."

"And," Wyatt picked up the story, "Mom secretly had a thing for him that whole time but refused to admit it."

"See," Flynn said, "my mom will like you just fine. Possibly even more than Wyatt."

"Hey, that's not true. She loves me. Who's the one who calls her every day? Is that you? No that's right, it's me."

"I'm not sure that as a grown ass man you should admit to calling your mom every day. That's a little disturbing."

"Fuck off."

Joy was laughing at their bickering which was way better than being upset that their mom might dislike her. "Wyatt, what do you do other than own this building?"

"I used to be a stockbroker, but got burned out. It's a stressful career and I refused to die young. So, instead, I use my skills to make my own money, and with Flynn's help, I run this building. I'm hoping to buy another building soon, maybe in a year or so."

"Wow, good for you for recognizing that being a stockbroker wasn't for you. Not everyone figures that out early."

"It was more Flynn and less me. He saw how bad I was and how I was killing myself trying to be the best. If not for him, I'd still be holed up in my office in New York, sucking on antacids twenty-four hours a day."

Joy looked over to him. "Flynn has a way of saving people, that's for sure."

"He's the best and I'm not just saying that because he's my brother."

"Can we maybe stop talking about me like I'm not here?"

"What fun would that be?"

"You just might be my new favorite person, Wyatt." Joy's face was covered in a huge smile.

"Hey," Flynn said, "Not cool."

"Sorry." She shrugged, laughing.

"I should get going," Wyatt said. "I still want to check the rest of the building and tenants to see if everyone is doing okay."

"Do you always do that?" Flynn asked, standing with Wyatt.

"No but after Joy's air went out, I thought I should be a more present building owner."

Slapping him on the back, Flynn opened the door. "I might be the better brother, but you are the better man."

Flynn meant those words. His brother was one of the best guys he knew and would do anything for anyone if he could. Shutting the door behind him, he turned to take in Joy who was still sitting on the couch.

"I like your brother."

"He's hard not to like." Leaning against the door, he closed his eyes. It had been a long two days and he was exhausted.

"Can you stay?"

His eyes flashed open. "Do you want me to stay?" This was a huge turn, her asking him for something.

"Always." She stood and walked toward him. Reaching around him, she locked her door. "Come on, let's go to bed."

Taking her hand he followed her as she turned off lights along their way. In her room, he sat on her bed and removed his shoes and shirt. He watched as Joy stripped out of her shorts and took her hair down from the crazy bun thingy on the top of her head.

"Sorry my bed's so small." He looked down and for the first time noticed that it was just a full size mattress.

"Small means I get to have you in my arms all night."

Moving to the top of the bed, she lowered the covers. "That is a bonus."

"I'll have to get up early so I can go back home and change before work." He set his phone on the nightstand, having already set the alarm.

"What's early?"

Shrugging he slid into bed. "Five."

Her eyes widened. "Five. In the morning. Holy hell, Flynn, I haven't been up at five in years."

"Sorry. It's the job and with Dax gone, I need to be there early to help load the trucks."

"I guess I can deal with it if it means I get to sleep with you in my bed." She scooted down and pulled the covers up over her.

Turning on his side, he pulled her close to his body. "I promise to make it worthwhile."

"Oh this sounds promising." She pushed her ass even closer to his already hardening cock.

Who needed sleep when you could have Joy?

Chapter 15

Joy woke up to an empty, cold bed where Flynn had slept. Glancing at her phone she saw it was just past seven. She also found a piece of paper that wasn't there the night before.

It was from Flynn.

Joy,

I didn't wake you even though I really wanted to. I hope you slept well, I know I did. Better than the previous two nights.

If you can, want to meet for dinner? Dockside at seven?

I already miss you,

Flynn

Hugging the note to her chest, she fell back on the bed. It was over for her. She was officially in love with Flynn. He'd come to her apartment, even after she'd practically ignored him for two days. He hadn't been willing to let her get away with pushing him out.

And boy, was she glad.

She'd just needed to see if she would be okay without him.

New flash.

She had not been okay.

She'd been miserable. It had been all she could do just to go to work and plaster a fake smile on her face. Forget eating or sleeping or enjoying anything about life.

She'd needed Flynn.

Flynn, who was sweet, hot, and sexy. Flynn, who knew she was scared of relationships, and grabbed her hand to steady her when he called her his girlfriend. Flynn, who made sure to tell her he loved the spaghetti she'd made, even though it was just spaghetti. Flynn, who fucked her so hard that she knew she'd be feeling him all day in everything she did.

It was all Flynn.

And she loved him.

Crazily enough, that thought wasn't freaking her out. And what's more, she wanted to tell him. And soon. He deserved to know how she felt.

The only problem was, she had no idea where to find him. If Dax and Avery were in town, she could find out easily enough from them, but she didn't know any of the other people who worked for him.

Wyatt. She could ask Wyatt.

Grabbing her phone, she texted the number he had given her when her air was out.

Joy:
Wyatt, this is Joy. Is there any chance you could find out where Flynn is for me? I need to tell him something and want to do it in person.
Wyatt:
As long as it's not bad news, count me in.
Joy:
It's definitely not bad news.

Minutes later, he texted her the address of where Flynn would be until noon. Since her first appointment wasn't until ten-thirty, she jumped up, showered and dressed. Once ready, she headed out the door. This might be the worst idea in the history of ideas, but she really wanted Flynn to know how she felt.

He was working at a building not too far from the center of town. Joy wasn't sure what it had previously been, but the sign outside said it was soon to be a nursery and landscape business.

She saw Flynn's truck, parking right next to it and hopped out. There looked to be about ten guys working on the place, but Flynn was nowhere in sight.

"Excuse me," she said to one of the guys, "do you know where I could find Flynn?"

The guy looked her up and down making her want to cringe. But, instead, she stood tall. Well, as tall as she could, for her short stature.

"I'm not sure, but is there something I could help you with?"

"No thanks, I really need Flynn for this." She started to walk away but could feel the guys eyes on her the whole time.

"Ah, come on," he said from behind her, "I'm just as good as Flynn."

"Joy?" She heard Flynn's voice from behind her too.

Turning she saw him standing next to the guy she'd been talking to.

"Is everything okay?" He looked at the guy who had been staring at her. "Mitch, don't you have some work to do?"

"Yeah, sorry boss."

"What's wrong?" He stepped forward gripping her hands.

"Nothing's wrong. I just wanted to see you."

"Was Mitch bothering you?"

"Not really, just being a typical guy."

"If he said something to you, I want you to tell me."

"It wasn't what he said, it was more how he looked at me. Like a piece of ass."

Flynn's face turned angry and she was pretty sure he growled. "I'll kill him."

"Please don't." She touched his chest. "It's just guys being guys."

"No, Joy, it's not. Guys should never make a woman feel afraid, or like a piece of ass, as you said. It's not right, and if it's not addressed, it will only keep happening. Men can admire a woman without making her feel like she is doing anything wrong."

Sighing, she leaned into him. "I love you, Flynn."

"What?" he held her away from him

"That's what I came here to tell you. I woke up alone and missing you, and I knew without a doubt that I loved you. Instead of being afraid or freaked out, all I wanted to do was tell you. Then you go and say something so amazing and sweet in defense of women everywhere, and my heart just fell all over again."

"You love me?"

"Yes you big idiot."

In an instant, he had her scooped up into his arms, both of them spinning in circles. He shouted out a loud "Whoop" before crashing his lips against hers. She held on to him for dear life as he continued to hold her up while kissing her.

"Can you put me down now?" She pursed her lips and tried to look annoyed.

"I'm never letting you down." He kissed her again, and this time, she heard claps from all around them.

"I'm starting to think that you get off on people watching us." Finally, he slid her down his body until her feet hit the ground.

"I like people to know that you are mine."

Shaking her head, she loosened her grip on his neck. "If I had to guess, news will get out fast now that you've kissed me at work."

"Is that a problem?"

"Not for me."

"Me neither." He pulled her close again, dropping his forehead to hers. "Tell me again?"

"I love you." It was surprisingly easy to say.

"God, I love you too. So fucking much."

"I should go." Even though she said the words, she didn't want to leave.

"We on for dinner?"

Nodding, she ran her fingers through his beard. "My last appointment is at six, so I might be a little late."

"I'll save you a seat."

Neither made a move to separate as they continued to stare at each other. A loud crash brought them both back to reality.

"See you later," she said, and kissed him lightly on the lips.

"I love you." His face held a huge smile.

"Love you too." She waved goodbye and walked out of the building. It felt so good to be honest, with not only Flynn, but with herself.

Also, what Flynn had said about how guys treat women was right. If you let them do it, the cycle would never be broken.

She was done with that.

Because she still had almost two hours before she needed to be at work, she drove to the center of town, where she just so happened to spot Julia's car in the lot in front of the coffee shop. Because she really wanted to talk to her, she parked and walked up to the sidewalk just as Julia was coming out.

"Hey," she said, "I was going to call you today."

"Now you don't have to."

"I take it from the very huge smile on your face that things with you and Flynn are going well? I'll tell you that scene at the wedding was hot. And that's my professional opinion."

"Things are great. Fantastic even. Although they almost weren't great."

"Uh oh, what happened?"

"Do you have a few minutes or are you in a hurry?"

"I've got time. No actual appointments until after lunch. I was just going to catch up on paperwork. But that can wait. Let's sit."

They found an empty table outside, and each took a seat. "Tell me what happened."

"Saturday and Sunday were amazing. Flynn is possibly the best guy in the whole world. But then Monday came and I got into my own head. I was so afraid that my happiness was because of him and I didn't want that. I thought that my happiness should come from me. I should be able to make myself happy without him. So I avoided him for two days."

"I'm gonna go ahead and assume that didn't go over well."

"You'd be correct. Thankfully, he's Flynn, and wouldn't let me give up on us. He showed up at my place and I could tell he was ready to fight for us, but by then, I'd already come to my senses and I jumped him as he came in the door."

"Nice. That's a classic move that tends to work a good percentage of the time."

"He definitely didn't push me away. But we talked and I admitted my happiness issues. It was a real breakthrough for me."

"Look at you, growing and learning. When you can see your own faults, that's a huge step."

"It's easier to retrain my brain than my heart. The heart wants to believe all the old bullshit that it learned early on."

"I get that. Just because I'm a therapist doesn't mean I didn't have my own hang-ups when it came to me and Wes. But like you, I let them go, and now I couldn't be happier."

"It's not easy, this love thing, that's for sure."

"You're in love with Flynn?" She set her coffee down, eyes wide.

"Oh did I forget to mention that?" She grinned, biting the side of her bottom lip.

"You might be the worst friend ever. You lead with that kind of info. Sex and declarations of love trump all other conversation."

"It just happened if it makes you feel any better."

"Did he say it first? You? Where were you?" Her hands were moving in furious motion. "Oh my God, I need all the information."

Laughing, Joy leaned back in her chair. "He told me he was more than halfway in love with me at the wedding, and then last night I asked him if that was true. To my surprise, he said no, but only because he was pretty much all the way in love with me."

"Ahh, I think I love Flynn a little. His body doesn't hurt."

"Hey married women, pay attention and stop picturing my boyfriend naked."

"Well, I wasn't picturing him fully naked, but I am now."

Joy rolled her eyes. "You know two can play at that game right? Wes is pretty hot in his own right."

Julia shrugged. "Go right ahead. I know who he's coming home to tonight."

Laughing, Joy shook her head. "Do you want to hear this or not?"

"Keep going. I can multitask."

"So there I am, knowing that he loves me and not sure what I think or feel. Except this morning I woke up to him already gone and a note. It was in that moment, while reading his note, that I knew I was completely in love with him. And more so, I wanted him to know. Immediately."

"That's why you're awake and out this early. I was wondering."

Giving her a *shut the fuck up look*, she kept going. "I texted his brother to see if he could find out where Flynn was."

"Whoa, Flynn as a brother?" Julia interrupted her.

"Yes, and he's crazy good looking. I'll get to that in a second. Anyway, Wyatt gets me Flynn's location and I head straight there finding him and declaring my love. Being Flynn, with his weird need to pick me up, he lifted me into his arms and kissed me silly." Her smile got bigger. "I told Flynn I loved him and didn't have a panic attack or freak out. And he loves me back."

"Congratulations, my friend, you have just entered into a whole new realm. And it looks good on you."

"It feels good too."

"Now that you're all healthy and functional, tell me about this good looking brother."

Laughing, Joy crossed her legs and told her friend all about Wyatt. Having friends made her almost as happy as being in love made her.

She was running later than she'd hoped to meet Flynn for dinner. Her last appointment had shown up more than twenty minutes late, and then hated the color she'd picked, meaning Joy had to redo it.

As if her bad color choosing skills were Joy's fault.

Some fucking people.

She'd texted Flynn as soon as she'd known she'd be late, and Flynn being Flynn, had texted back "I'd wait forever for you."

She swooned.

Something that was totally new and foreign to her.

Stepping into Dockside, she spotted him immediately, sitting at the bar talking to Sabrina and the chef, Patrick.

"Hey," she said as she walked up behind him.

"There's my girl." Flynn said, and stood like the gentleman he was.

Grabbing her waist, he pulled her into his body and kissed her. "Longest day ever," he whispered.

"It looks like that first date, which was right here at my bar, might I add, was successful." At Sabrina's voice, Joy lifted her head.

"Don't get cocky." She sat in the bar stool that Flynn had pulled out for her.

"I didn't even know this was happening," Patrick said. "Being back in the kitchen means I miss a lot."

"It's new," Joy said.

"It may be new, but it's been a long time coming," Sabrina added, "and, I for one, am happy for you both."

Sabrina and Patrick walked away, leaving her alone with Flynn.

"Sorry your day ran long." His fingers entwined with hers on the bar.

Shrugging, she said, "What are you gonna do. How was the rest of your day?"

"It was good, after I had a talk with my guys about treating women right."

"You did what now?" She turned fully to look at him.

"I can't stand by and let people knowingly treat you, or any woman, as anything other than equals. It's not in me to sit idle and watch that."

"Great, now all the guys who work for you think I'm a bitch."

"Not true. I had several guys come to me and say they've heard and seen the way that Mitch treats women, and they were glad I said something. They felt uncomfortable, but were afraid to step up and say something."

"What about Mitch, how did he react?"

"Not great at first. Said some bullshit about that was how the world was, and that it was just flirting. I then explained that flirting didn't include making a woman feel like a piece of meat, and that if he wanted to keep his job, he needed to change his ways."

Dropping her head into her hand, she groaned. "So now I'm responsible for someone losing their job."

"First, you are not responsible for anything. If a guy disrespects a woman, that's on him. Second, Mitch broke down and explained that he and his girlfriend of three years had just broken up and he was devastated. He's been hanging out with a bunch of single guys who troll the bars every night, and while he didn't think it was right, when they spoke to women like that, they got laid."

Sighing, she picked her head back up. "Yeah, I guess I can see that. Six months ago, I was that girl who would have been okay with that."

He leaned in, kissing her lightly on the lips. "Now you're stronger, wiser, and all mine."

She ran her fingers through his beard. God she loved the feel of doing that. "I like myself so much better now. Especially, the "being yours part."

"No making out at the bar!" Sabrina shouted from the other side of the bar.

"How fast can you eat?" Flynn asked, completely serious.

"No way, I am hungry and want to spend time with you that's not in the bedroom." She let him go and picked up the drink that sat in front of him.

"I'm flexible. We, in no way, have to do it in a bed."

"Yeah, you proved that last night." She set the beer back down.

"If memory serves me right, you said you liked that."

There was heat in his eyes. Heat that told her he was remembering – just like she was – how hot the over the arm of the couch sex had been.

If he kept looking at her like that, she was going to willingly starve just to do it again.

"Stop. I need food."

Laughing, he picked up his beer and took a long swallow. "It's your fault. Stop being so sexy and I will stop wanting you." He frowned. "Yeah, no, that's not gonna work either because I love your mind more than I love your body. I'm thinking, we're fucked."

He was probably right. There didn't seem to be much talking going on when they were together.

They ordered food, which he had waited to do until she got there, and spent the next hour chatting as they ate. When the food was gone, Patrick stopped by to ask how everything was.

"It was great." Flynn said. "Did you cook or is Wes back there?"

"He's cooking tonight. I'm working out here and then taking over for him soon, so he can go home."

"Do you have any cupcakes left?" Joy asked. "Those things are like crack. Not that I've ever done crack, so really I have no idea if they are like crack. Oh, they're like Flynn...once you get a taste you never want to give them up."

"Nice analogy," Flynn said smiling.

"I'm gonna have to take your word on that one," Patrick said, "but yes, we still have some cupcakes. While I've never met this elusive Dani who makes them, she is a cupcake God."

"I've only met her once," Joy said. "She's a sweet girl with big dreams."

"There's no doubt she'll get those dreams if they have anything to do with these cupcakes." Patrick slipped one onto a plate and slid it to her. "Enjoy."

"Wanna share?" she asked Flynn.

"What do you think the chances are of us getting several of these cupcakes to take home with us?"

There was a gleam in his eyes. "Are you insinuating that we should eat these cupcakes while in bed?"

"Again, I'm okay with the couch or the floor."

She slapped his arm, but at the same time shouted, "Patrick, can I get several more cupcakes please?"

Flynn may have come up with the idea, but she was going to do her damnedest to follow through with creativity.

Calories be damned.

Chapter 16

"No." Flynn had been listening to his brother try to convince him for over an hour, to invest in a building in town.

"Come on, man, it's a good deal."

"It is a good deal, but I'm not willing to part with that kind of money right now."

"But it's money you wouldn't even have if it weren't for me."

Years ago, Flynn had put Wyatt in charge of his finances since he was a whiz with all that stuff. Wyatt had done his job and made him plenty of money, for which Flynn was thankful. But, after his house and the apartment building he'd already purchased with him, he was ready to be done with investments.

Not to mention, now that he was with Joy, they might need that money for their future.

"And I thank you for that, but I just don't want to spend any of it right now. I might need it."

"Let me guess, for Joy?"

"Maybe. Why's that matter?"

He sighed. "It doesn't. I like Joy. A lot."

"That's a good thing since I love her."

His head snapped up. "That was fast."

"Not really. She's been it for me since the day I met her."

"Mom says I'm not supposed to give you shit about her because this is the real deal, but seriously, when did I ever agree to not giving you shit?"

"I see you ran right out and told mom you met her. Same old Wyatt." He was kidding, of course, because everyone in their family knew that Wyatt talked to mom every day. They were more like friends and less like parent and child.

"She says you better bring her home soon or else she's dragging dad here for a visit." He raised his eyebrows. "But I did tell her that Joy is awesome, although, I also said I have no idea what she's doing with you."

"I'll remember this conversation when you fall in love."

"Never gonna happen. There's no one out there who can match me."

"You mean there's no one out there who can put up with you." Flynn stood up from the table where he'd been sitting talking to Wyatt. "I gotta get back to work." He threw some cash on the table. "I'm sorry I can't help you with the building. Maybe next time."

"Yeah, yeah, go ahead and be responsible and save your money for your future."

Flynn walked out laughing, waving a goodbye to Wes who was behind the bar. Wyatt had called him that morning and asked to meet. Flynn never refused his brother and was able to carve out some time during lunch. He'd spent both Wednesday and Thursday night with Joy, and they had plans again that night. Although, he had invited Wyatt since all they were doing was going to Addison and Ryan's for game night. He had declined, saying he did not want to be the third wheel.

Or, in this case, the seventh wheel, since Carly and Tony were also joining them.

He worked for four more hours, cutting out early since his guys were ahead of schedule. Both he and Dax liked to work hard throughout the week so they could let their crews go early, if possible, on Fridays. And shockingly, even with Dax gone on his honeymoon, they had managed to stay ahead of schedule.

When he pulled into his driveway, he saw Joy's car already parked there. While he didn't mind that she was there—he'd given her the entry code—he was supposed to pick her up at six. Entering his house, he called out her name, but there was no answer. Dropping his keys and phone on the counter, he kept walking, but didn't see her in the living room either. As he approached his room, he saw the door was closed. Pushing it open, his breath caught when he saw Joy lying on his bed.

She was wearing some sort of lingerie, but really, it barely covered her. And it was red. Cherry red.

And so were her lips.

And the pose she was in left nothing to the imagination.

He got hard in the blink of an eye.

"Is this...okay?" The unsure sound of her voice rang out in the room.

He swallowed and took a step forward. "Are you fucking kidding me? Is it my birthday or Christmas? What in the world did I do to deserve this?"

Smiling, she opened her legs even wider. "You love me."

"That's an every day, every minute thing. This," he licked his lips, "is a very special occasion thing."

"To me, they're one and the same. Now stop stalling and come over here and get your present."

"Honey, as good as that sounds, I am dirty and in desperate need of a shower."

"Sounds good to me." She slid from the bed to stand.

He wasn't a dummy and was not planning on turning down shower sex. "When we get out, will you promise to put this back on?"

"That depends."

"On what?"

"On how well you do in the shower." She walked into his bathroom leaving him staring at her ass which was bare thanks to a thong.

He gripped his harder than steel cock, squeezing it to try to find some control.

It didn't work. He heard the shower start and instantly he got into motion shedding his clothing as he went to join her. He was naked, his cock bobbing against his stomach, when he finally saw her again, this time naked.

"Listen, we've had a lot of sex this week, but I don't think that's going to make a difference in speed. I can't fucking get enough of you, especially when I come home from work to find you seducing me in my bed."

"Stop talking and get in the shower."

He blinked at her aggressiveness, his dick twitching at the anticipation of her being in charge.

Stepping forward, he skimmed his fingers along the naked skin of her stomach and stepped into the already running shower. Her hand landed on his ass as she climbed in right behind him, caressing it gently, then slapping it hard.

Never in his life did he think he'd like that, but with Joy, it seemed he was a new man.

He reached for the soap but she took it out of his hands before he could use it.

"Let me," she said, running the soap over his shoulders and down his back. Her hands trailed around to his stomach and the tips of her fingers just barely grazed the head of his cock. He wanted to drop to his knees and beg her to speed up, to touch him.

He tried to turn to face her, but she was having none of that. "Stay like this." Her hand traveled higher, the bar of soap scrapping over his ribs, and then grazing his nipples, making him hiss out a breath.

"Joy." His voice was hoarse from arousal.

"Just relax and enjoy." Her lips moved against his back, water cascading down over both of them.

A harsh laugh escaped. "Relaxing while you're touching me is impossible."

"Try harder." Her hands went lower, back down his stomach.

He held his breath, hoping and praying she would finally touch his dick. Slowly, he felt the bar of soap run down the length of him before it was gone and just her hand remained. She stroked him up and down twice before her hand went lower and massaged his balls. The soap was washing away just as fast as it touched him thanks to the water that fell over them.

He wanted to let her continue, wanted her to have her control. But, his need to see her and touch her, trumped all that.

Spinning quickly, he gripped her ass and pulled her into his body, his cock nestled between them. "You are fucking killing me," he whispered against her ear.

"What are you going to do about it?" A mischievous smile appeared on her face.

So, this was all a ploy to have him fuck her hard. She didn't want control, she wanted him to be a caveman.

That he could fucking do.

Pushing her up against the tiled shower wall, he kissed, licked, and bit his way down her shoulders to her breasts. He could feel her heart pounding under his mouth and hands as his tongue flicked over her nipple.

When she wrapped her legs around his waist, he pushed harder to hold her against the wall. Her nails were dragging up and down his back as her hips gyrated against his erection.

One of her hands traveled between their bodies, her small fingers gripping his cock.

"Please," she begged, and there was no way he could deny her. Not when he wanted the same thing.

But, just before he pushed inside her, he remembered the condom.

"Shit, shit, shit." He dropped his head on her shoulder.

"Why are you stopping?" She grabbed his hair and forced his head up to look at her.

"I don't have a condom in here." He started to lower her legs to the ground. "I'll go get one."

She tightened her legs around his waist and smiled. "I'm on the pill."

His eyes searched hers. "That's a big step." He'd never had sex without a condom, honestly, he had never wanted to. There had even been a few times where the woman had said she'd been on the pill, but he'd always still used a condom.

Accidents happened and he'd wanted no part of that.

But with Joy, he knew she was his future, and the thought of being bare inside her, was a major turn on.

"A step I've never taken before," she said, her fingers playing with his beard like they always did.

Her admission told him everything he needed to know. They were on the same page of the same book. A book that ended in happily ever after.

Slowly—well as slow as he could go, considering how good it felt—he pushed inside her. The feeling alone was enough to send him over the edge, but the look on her face, pure ecstasy and happiness, had him more than halfway there.

Pausing once fully inside her, he took several steadying breaths. It was too much, too good, and he wanted it to last.

But when she said, "Don't worry, we have our whole lives to do this," he broke. He wasn't sure if it was the fact that she'd known what he'd been thinking, or that she had basically just said she'd be with him forever, either way though, he didn't care.

All he wanted was her.

He began pumping into her, their bodies equally racing toward the feeling of euphoria that only came when they were together. Her moans and breathless pants spurred him on as his own echoed off the walls.

She felt so good, like home, and he never wanted to leave her.

As she shattered around him, he let himself go and pumped furiously into her, spilling everything he had.

It was possibly the best feeling he'd had in recent memory.

Other than the day she'd told him she loved him.

She lifted her head to look at him, a smile curving her lips. "Can we do that again?"

Laughing, he lowered her feet to the floor, slipping out of her as he did so. "We are most definitely doing that again."

Stepping back he quickly rinsed off and pulled her to him to do the same. After toweling dry, she started to get dressed when he stopped her.

"Excuse me, but didn't you promise to put that," he pointed to her lingerie on the floor, "back on?"

"You really want me to?" She raised her eyebrows in question. "We have to be at Addison and Ryan's in an hour."

He bent down, picking up the scrap of lace. "That gives us just enough time, don't you think?" He handed her the skimpy material.

Taking it from him, she smirked. "I want you to remember this moment in a few months, when you are too tired for sex."

He scoffed. "That's a myth. Guys are never too tired for sex."

"You can't tell me that it will always be like this. Us, not being able to keep our hands off each other."

"I can't predict the future, but I do know that I will never tire of touching you, or being with you." At her look of doubt he asked, "Look at Leah and Brandon or Carly and Tony. Hell, any of our friends. None of them can keep their hands to themselves. Or their lips."

She pursed her lips. "I guess, but that can't be the norm, can it?"

He reached out putting his hands on her shoulders. "I think that real love, all consuming, raw love, makes you want that person all the time. And that's us, or at least it's me."

"It's me too," she said, biting her bottom lip, "and I want that...what our friends have."

"You have it." He leaned in to kiss her, which led them to the bed which, in turn, led them to making love.

They ended up being thirty minutes late to Addison and Ryan's, but all the jokes at their expense were one hundred percent worth it.

Chapter 17

When she woke up Saturday morning she stretched her body, sore in places it had never been sore before. Turning her head, she found Flynn still asleep next to her, his soft breathing making his chest rise and fall.

He was so handsome, it took her breath away.

Sometimes, there was still a part of her brain that didn't understand why he loved her. But, each day, that part was getting smaller and smaller with every I love you, and every sweet kiss or touch.

In a way, it felt weird to be happy, partly because it was a totally foreign emotion for her but, she was learning.

And having Flynn made it that much easier.

Yawning, she turned on her side and snuggled into Flynn. He moved, his arm coming around her head.

"For someone who likes her sleep, you are always the first one awake."

She smiled against his chest. She did like her sleep. Before meeting Flynn, she rarely got up before eight. For some strange reason though, now she awoke early.

"I guess I just like to spend more time with you."

"I will never complain about that."

They came back to his house after their game night with their friends. It was silly to go to her apartment when he had his own house. And he had the bigger bed which gave them more room to move.

"I hate that I have to work today and you don't." She'd never in her life hated working on Saturdays or Sundays, but now it sucked. All she wanted to do was spend her time with Flynn.

"It's only a few hours, and I'll be here when you get off so we can do something fun together."

"I'll hold you to that."

He rolled on top of her. "How much time do you have before you have to leave?"

She laughed and ran her hands up and down his back. "I think I can fit you in."

An hour later, she was in her car on her way to Woodridge, where she had a wedding party to take care of for the next four hours. She had two other girls helping her with both mani's and pedi's.

The whole time she worked, her mind was on Flynn. He made her feel so good, not only about herself, but about their future. While they were at Addison and Ryan's the night before, conversation, of course, turned to babies, because both Addison and Carly were pregnant. It was the first time in her life that she'd ever contemplated having kids. She'd never wanted kids. Never thought she could be a good mom. But, sitting there listening to her friends talk about babies and how ill prepared they felt, made her realize that most people probably thought they would be a shitty parent.

While she might feel that way about herself, she knew, without a doubt, that Flynn would be a fantastic father. Reed, who was Carly's seven-year-old brother and Reed's nephew, had been there, and Flynn seemed to enjoy hanging out and playing with him. Several times she'd looked out into the living room to find him enthralled in something with Reed.

It made her heart flip flop in her chest.

Something that had never happened to her before.

Then. when they'd gotten back to his house and he'd made slow, sensual love to her, making her feel like the most cherished person in the world.

Now all she wanted was...well everything.

If it involved Flynn.

She wasn't sure whether to hate him or love him more for making her feel this way.

When the wedding party was finished with their pampering, she drove back to Cedarville, stopping in town to pick up a few items at the grocery store. When she was finished shopping, she was putting her bags in her car when she spotted Wyatt.

"Hey, Wyatt!" she shouted and waved.

He jogged over. "Joy, how's it going?"

"Good. Just on my way back to Flynn's now that work is over. What are you up to?"

"I was checking out a building I'm thinking about purchasing."

"Oh really, which one?"

"The small one between the bookstore and the liquor store." He pointed over to the empty space.

Immediately her thoughts turned to how perfect that would be for her. "What would you do with it?"

"Rent it out. Property is a great investment and brings in money long term. While I like the apartment building, this would be a lot less work."

She bit her lip and wondered if there was any way she'd be able to come up with enough money for the monthly rent. Actually that was the least of her problems. The start-up costs alone would be more than she could afford.

Maybe she could take out a loan.

"I have to get going, I'm meeting with the realtor. Tell Flynn I say hi."

She waved, her mind still trying to process the possibility of how she could open her own nail salon. Sliding into her car, she pondered what she'd need for start up. It was time to make a list and add up costs.

Only she wasn't sure she had enough business sense to do it on her own.

Flynn's house came into view and she spotted him outside working in the yard.

Shirtless.

Immediately all thoughts of the salon went out the window.

He looked up when she pulled in the drive, lifting a hand in hello. He was walking toward her as she stepped out of her car.

"Hey, babe." He held the door open.

"What are you up to?" She perused his half naked form, absently licking her lips.

"Catching up on my landscaping." He took the bags she pulled from the car. "What'd you get?" He looked into the bags.

"I thought maybe we could grill out tonight or tomorrow so I picked up some steaks and veggies to grill."

His eyes widened. "Really? I love steak."

"I know, you told me." She smiled, shutting the car door. It was one of those facts he'd told her the first time they'd met. She recalled it when she woke up that morning and figured why not give him something he loved?

"I was pretty sure I couldn't love you more, but this changes the game."

Walking, he followed her as they went into his house. "You are easy to please if steak makes you this happy."

"You make me this happy," he said, and dropped the bags on the counter. Reaching for her, he pulled her into his arms. "I missed this."

"You just saw me this morning." She secretly loved that he always seemed to miss her when she was away.

"That was too many hours ago." He nuzzled her neck, sending shivers through her body.

"That tickles," she giggled, trying to wiggle away from him.

"Looks like I found your weakness." He continued to rub his beard against her neck, making her laugh the whole time.

Finally, she wiggled free, taking a step back. "You stay over there."

He smiled and winked at her, but then began unpacking her bags.

"I ran into Wyatt in town."

"In Woodridge?"

"No, here in Cedarville, when I stopped at the store." She sat on a stool. "He was looking at a building that he said he's thinking of buying."

"Oh yeah, he told me about that. Wanted me to go in on it with him."

"Are you?"

"I told him no, that right now I don't want to use my money for that."

"Hmm." She rested her chin on her fist.

Flynn closed the refrigerator and looked at her. "Something up?"

She pursed her lips, wondering if she should tell Flynn what she'd been thinking. He already knew she wanted her own salon, so it wasn't that big a deal.

"It just made me think that maybe I could rent it from him for a salon."

"That would be a great idea." The genuine happiness lit up his eyes.

"It would be, but I'm not sure I'm ready yet, or that I have the money for the start-up costs.." She could see by the change in his eyes that he was about to say something she wasn't going to like. "Don't." She put a hand up to stop him. "I can't and won't take your money. This is something I have to do myself."

He sighed. "I know that and I respect it. I just want you to have everything you want in the world."

"And I appreciate that, and love you for it, but I need to prove to myself that I can do this."

"I have no doubt that you can do this. Just remember though...a lot of people have help when they start out. That doesn't make you weak or bad. It makes you smart." He opened a bottle of water. "If Dax hadn't taken a chance on me when I moved here, who knows what would have happened. I was a kid fresh out of college with no real experience. But, he saw something in me, and now I'm his second in charge."

"Do you ever think about going out on your own?"

"I did, for like a minute. But, I know that I would need a good right-hand man, and those are hard to find. Dax pays me well, and as a bonus, he is the one that gets the middle of the night calls."

Smiling, she took the bottle of water out of his hand. "I'm glad that it's not because you think you couldn't do it. Because you could." She took a sip of water, twisted the cap back on. "Now, I'm pretty sure that this morning when I left for work, you promised me some fun tonight."

"That I did." He came around the counter, moving between her already opened legs. "What would you say to dinner at Dockside and then we hit the festival over at the Catholic Church?"

"A church festival? I haven't done that since I was a kid." She pulled him in closer, licked his bottom lip with her tongue. "Can we maybe add to this plan of yours?" She felt his hands grip her hips.

"You can have anything you want." When his lips crashed against hers, she moaned thinking she already did.

Two hours, and several orgasms later, they arrived at Dockside for dinner. The place was packed as it usually was on weekends, but they found Melanie, Logan, Leah, and Brandon, already sitting at a table and joined them.

"Hey, I expected you awhile ago," Brandon said to Flynn, scooting over so there was more room.

Flynn looked at her, biting his lip with a gleam in his eyes. "Yeah, we kinda got distracted."

"Been there," Melanie said, and high-fived Joy. "That is the only legitimate excuse for being late."

A waitress came over and took their drink order, both of them ordering a beer. Before it came though, she excused herself to go and say hi to Wes. They hadn't had a whole lot of time to talk since she and Flynn had started dating, and she felt guilty for abandoning her friend.

She found him in the kitchen, hair net on his head, making burgers.

"If it isn't my crazy friend, Joy," he said as he continued to work.

"Don't be an ass." She pulled out the stool that he left back there for Julia. "How's life?"

"Pretty damn good." He was smiling as he continued to work. "I have everything I've ever wanted. It feels good." He plated the burgers, turning toward her. "How are you? Flynn and you seem pretty close."

"I love him." It came out so easy that she even surprised herself.

"I kinda assumed that when he carried you out of the wedding. You wouldn't have let just anyone do that."

Pursing her lips she thought about that. Had she been that obvious? "Is it supposed to feel this...big?"

"Yes, dummy it is. Love should consume you. It should also make you feel settled; calm."

"Well then, I'm at least doing it right. I've never been this calm in my life."

"I like Flynn. A lot. And I like you guys together."

Thinking of Flynn and how happy he made her, she smiled. "He loves me, even with all my issues, and crazy." She shook her head. "Some days I wonder why."

"You're one of the best people I know, Joy, so it doesn't surprise me at all that he loves you."

She bit her bottom lip. "He wants to give me the money to start my own salon." Sure, he hadn't said the actual words, but she knew he would have if she hadn't stopped him from speaking.

Wes didn't bat an eyelash. "That's amazing!"

"Wes, I can't take his money."

"Why the hell not? You guys are in love, you're going to build a future together. Take the damn money and start your business."

"That's easy for you to say. You already have your business."

"Yeah, and do you know why I have my business? Because my wife, the love of my life, loaned me the money. Don't be stupid, Joy. The man loves you and wants to help you. If you're going to build a life with him, why not start now?"

She hated when he made good points; hated that he was right. "Isn't it too soon to be talking about building a life together? We just started dating."

"Take it from someone who lost a lot of time with the person he loved, don't wait a minute if you love him. Time waits for no man, or in this case woman."

Standing, she gave him a hug. "Let's have breakfast one day next week."

"You're on," he said and she walked out the door and back into the restaurant.

She still wasn't sure about taking the money from Flynn, but she had an idea. One she hoped he'd go for.

Chapter 18

After dinner, they walked the four blocks to where the church festival was happening, Leah and Brandon joining them. Mel and Logan claimed they needed to get home for their dog, but Flynn suspected from the looks and touches they were giving each other at dinner, that they really just wanted to get home and go to bed.

Not for sleep.

He'd like to do the same with Joy, but he'd promised her fun, and really, could they spend all their time in bed?

That was a dumb question. Of course they could.

Or at least he could. She might need a few breaks.

Walking hand-in-hand, they played a few games, rode a few rides, and ate way too much sugar in the form of funnel cakes, candy apples, and ice cream. She and Leah laughed as he and Brandon went head-to-head trying to win them each stuffed animals, but were shown up by a twelve-year old.

It hurt more for Brandon, since it was a shooting game, even if it was just a water gun.

"Thanks for trying." Joy stood up on her toes, kissing his lips.

"I feel like a total failure."

"You?" Brandon said. "That kid crushed me and I'm the chief of police."

"Really though, babe," Leah said, "how often do you shoot your gun."

"I go to the range a couple times a month."

"Maybe you should go more," Joy joked.

"Don't listen to her." Leah pulled his face down to hers. "You don't need any practice."

As they kissed, Flynn took Joy's hand again. "Ready to get out of here?"

"Sure. You promised me fun and I'd say we had a lot of it."

Pulling on her hand, she came close to him and he took advantage by kissing her. "I have a lot more fun in store for when we get home."

"I bet you do."

After walking back to Dockside to grab his truck, they drove to his place, Joy blaring the music and singing loudly. He loved her in all her moods, but when she was carefree and happy, he loved her the most.

He parked and was about to get out of the truck when she placed her hand on his leg to stop him.

"I've been thinking..."

"Yeah?"

"I can't take your money, Flynn, as much as I'd love to have my salon sooner, I just can't. But there is something I could do to save a ton of money."

"What is it? I'd do anything to help."

"What if," she paused, biting her bottom lip. "What if we lived together?"

He wasn't sure he'd heard her correctly at first. Had she said live together? Was she reading his mind?

"Say something."

"Joy," he said her name and then took a deep breath. "I would have had you move in the day I met you, if I thought you'd have gone for it. I love you. You are it for me. So, living together was also a given for me."

She let out a breath she'd been holding. "Oh, thank God. I thought I was going to freak you out."

"Nothing you say or do will freak me out, unless you leave me. Please don't leave me."

"I wouldn't. Couldn't." She reached for his hand, squeezed it in hers. "On the outside, I pretended I didn't want this, didn't want love. But secretly, it's all I thought about. I wanted someone to love me for me, but even more, I wanted to love someone with my whole heart. You are that person for me."

He hated that they were in his truck. He wanted to hold her, kiss her, and tell her over and over how much he loved her. Opening his door, he quickly jumped out and ran around to her side, ripping her door open. Gripping her, he pulled her out of the truck and to him.

"I love you so much. I waited my whole life to find you, and when I did, I could never get you out of my mind. And now that I have you, I want nothing else but to be with you day in and day out." He saw her eyes glistening with tears, and because he knew she'd hate that, he kissed her.

And kissed her.

And kissed her some more.

"You can count on me, Joy. Forever. I will never let you down, and I will always love you."

The tears were still there, but there was also a smile on her face. "I know I can. That's why I know this is real. Right." She swiped at her eyes. "But, I want you to know that you can count on me, too. I want to be the person you come to when things go wrong as well as when they are right."

"You already are that person." He dropped his forehead against hers. "Let's start our life together now. Move in with me, love me, and be mine forever?"

He felt like it was forever before she answered, when in reality, it was barely a second.

"Yes." A huge, brilliant smile turned up her lips. "Yes to it all."

That moment, when the woman he loved, who also loved him, gave him everything he'd ever wanted, would go down as the best day of his entire life.

Also by Bree Kraemer
The Only Series
Only By His Touch
Only With Trust
If Only
Only You
Only For Love
Cedarville Novels
An Unexpected Home
Capturing Us
Choosing You
Better Together
A Chance Worth Taking
Forever Starts Here
After All These Years
Won't Let You Down
Say When
Something to Lose
Finally Home
Friends & Brothers
Sky High Love
Bridge To Love
When It's Love
Rockstar Romance
The Right Note
Pick Me
Christmas Novella
Light Me Up
DecorHATE for the Holidays
The Beckmeyer Family
Hooked
Sparked
Shocked
Kneaded
Valley Falls Strikers
Late Tackle
First Touch
Give & Go
Narrowing the Angle

He's a Keeper
Ground Rule
Walk Off
Sacrifice Bunt
Grand Slam (April 2023)